GHOSTS OF THE
SAN JUAN

BY DONALD WILLERTON

Ghosts of the San Juan

GHOSTS OF THE SAN JUAN

A MOGI FRANKLIN MYSTERY
BOOK 1

DONALD WILLERTON

WISE WOLF
BOOKS

Ghosts of the San Juan
Paperback Edition
Copyright © 2024 (As Revised) Donald Willerton

Wise Wolf Books
An imprint of Wolfpack Publishing

wisewolfbooks.com

Paperback ISBN 978-1-965596-31-9
eBook ISBN 978-1-965596-30-2

For My Mother

GHOSTS OF THE SAN JUAN

CHAPTER 1

THE SAN JUAN RIVER, NAVAJO COUNTRY, SOUTHERN UTAH, APRIL 1934

Not long after dawn, as the sunlight crept down the imposing rock faces of the deep, narrow canyon, four men in two home-made boats were swept along in the muddy current of the San Juan River. Within a short time, three of them would be dead and the fourth would be surprised by how easy it was to let them die.

But that would be later.

On this day, the leader of the expedition sat in the front boat, watching the canyon ahead with images flooding back into his mind. Somewhere ahead of him was a solid sandstone mesa hundreds of feet tall —flat-topped, steep-sided, and surrounded by nothing but a rugged canyon of rocks, cactus, and sagebrush. Disconnected from the regular wall of cliffs lining the river's corridor, the mesa sat isolated, an ultimately lonely mile-long piece of rock.

Hours passed until the man finally glimpsed it and smiled. His many years as a geologist, more years than he liked to remember, had until now provided only enough living to get by. Within a few days, if everything went the way he had been dreaming for the last year, he'd never have to worry about money again.

When the boats reached the foot of the towering piece of sandstone, the men pulled them to the bank and tied them to a tree.

———

A rope cinched around his body, Gordon Kattrick pulled himself up by his elbows, swung his waist and legs up and over the edge, and rolled onto the flat of the rock step, streams of sweat running from his brows into his eyes. He squinted from the burn. Rubbing his eyes to ease the pain only ground in the grit and sweat from his hands, making them burn even more.

Disgusted and blinded, he shucked his pack, pulled out his shirttail, and wiped his face.

Southern Utah was an immense, confusing land of twisted canyons and tilted mesas. It was as if thick, cream-colored cake frosting had been smeared in layers over hundreds of square miles of earth, then sculpted with a butter knife to make swirls, dips, and slices. But it was solid rock instead of cake frosting, and the swirls, dips, and slices made up a vast empire of mountains, winding valleys, gullies, canyons, and tall, isolated buttes.

This part of the canyon of the San Juan River was even more extreme than the rest of the countryside. Cutting through up to two thousand feet of layered rock, the river had created a steep-sided channel that twisted and turned for almost a hundred miles. Water erosion over millions of years had made ledges in the canyon walls as pieces of rock sheared off and fell into the river below. A series of large steps from the bottom halfway up each side made the walls resemble a multi-layered wedding cake, each layer made up of a flat rock shelf bumping up against a vertical piece of sandstone behind it.

The sides of the isolated mesa were no different. Tying the rope to a large boulder half-buried in the sand and dirt, Kattrick looked around him. They had struggled up four of the ledges, he now stood on the fifth. He had to be getting close to what he was searching for. Hurried by the thought, he kicked at the sagebrush and sand along the bottom of the ledge wall in front of him until, a few yards later, he found what he wanted.

Behind him, grumbling at him for not lending a hand to help, the three other men fought to pull themselves up by the rope onto the ledge, brushing themselves off as they stood. Then they stepped through the loose rocks, gravel, and sand to see why their leader was whooping and shouting. Not sharing his enthusiasm for rocks nor his obvious passion for hard work, they watched him quietly.

Kattrick was greedily pulling at a bush covering an opening at the bottom of the ledge wall. The opening was maybe two feet across, two and a half feet high. Perhaps it had once been an isolated split in the rock, or a hole left by a chunk of sandstone that had fallen out, or even a small animal's hole made large by water. Whatever its beginning, his efforts revealed that the opening led to a tunnel disappearing into the cliff.

Kattrick stood up and turned to the men. With his eyes on the youngest and smallest, he nodded toward the hole.

"Get inside there and see what you find."

"Hey, wait a minute—why me? There're probably snakes in there! I'm not going in that hole, no way!" J.D. gave Little Jake a swat on the head and pushed him toward the opening. "The way you smell, you'll scare 'em off. Now quit bellyaching and do as he says." J.D. figured that if Jake refused to do it, he'd be the next pick, and there was no way he was going into that hole first. There might be snakes.

Waiting for the bickering to end, Kattrick looked over the edge and down the mesa wall that they had just climbed. A smoothly carved path at his feet showed the years of wear by water flowing out from the tunnel, cascading onto each ledge below until it poured into a big pool in the canyon floor. It was in the pool that he had found the stones.

A year ago, an oil company had hired him to map the geology of this section of the San Juan canyon. Sweating in the miserable heat, drawing diagrams of the mesa's different sandstone layers, he had stopped to sift through a catch basin where rain poured off in huge waterfalls from the ledges above. Fingering a handful of gravel, he immediately recognized several stones whose deep, translucent reds and glassy greens made them stand out against the motley mixture of browns, blacks, yellows, and grays.

Kattrick's face flushed red, and his throat went dry.

Stones like these were only found close to lava eruptions, and the chances of finding other, more valuable, stones like diamonds, rubies, and sapphires were high. He had obviously run across some kind of eruption site hidden under the sandstone layers of the mesa.

Going through several more handfuls in the pool, Kattrick bagged the best of the stones and slipped them into his back pocket. They needed to be analyzed. If an eruption site could be found, it would be worth more than all the oil anyone would ever pump out of this godforsaken canyon. And since he was unlikely to ever get a cut of any oil profits, he'd keep the discovery of the stones to himself.

Kattrick had been dreaming of his return trip ever since.

Grudgingly defeated, Little Jake lit his lantern, got down on his knees, and squirmed headfirst into the tunnel, pushing the light ahead of him, cursing all the way.

"I didn't sign up for this," he shouted back, slithering on his stomach, scraping his elbows and knees on what felt like coarse sandpaper.

In a few feet, the tunnel grew large enough for him to move to a kneeling position and then to stand stooped over. The passage snaked back and forth, growing taller and wider. The smell of his sweat mixed with the stink of the lantern made him feel like puking.

The tunnel turned sharply upward. In the lantern's dim light, running his hands across the rock floor as it arched up in front of him, he had trouble believing what he saw.

Jake twisted around and moved back in a hurry, yelling back through the hole. "Hey, you gotta see this! Come on in, it's a lot bigger once you get past the entrance."

Kattrick, J.D., and Bob lit their lanterns and started their own grunting and squirming. If Jake had hated the cramped space, Navajo Bob was terrified. Snakes do holes, not people. This tunnel might be a trap set by Coyote, the Navajo trickster. Bob had agreed to get Kattrick to the remote mesa since he was Navajo and might be handy if they got into a scrape on the reservation. And Bob also knew how to handle the boats.

But crawling into a hole wasn't part of the deal.

Sweat dripping onto the floor as he squirmed through the opening, Navajo Bob tried to think of himself entering his family's hogan south of Mexican Hat. Feeling this image, breathing deeply and whispering a chant against evil spirits, he inched forward behind the others.

Finding Little Jake, Kattrick moved to the upsweep in the passageway, knelt, and ran his hands inside the depressions. Even in the flickering light of the lanterns, it was obvious.

"These are steps! It's a damn stairway!"

About half a dozen chipped-out depressions a foot or so apart ran up the curving rock. The steps were old and worn by the water through the years, but the regularity couldn't be missed. It was no work of nature.

The geologist, his eyes wild with discovery, crowded Little Jake aside and jammed his boots into the depressions, rashly hurrying up into the darkness. The strangeness of the tunnel was bewildering—the swirling patterns in the surrounding rock, the footholds, the darkness, and the thick, wet air. A moment later, he felt a whisper of breeze on his ear. He turned his lantern's wick up and watched the smoke it made move up the passageway. A breeze in the tunnel meant another opening was ahead.

Rounding a bend, a gray haze shone in the tunnel, a light of some sort. Coming up the last footholds, Kattrick climbed into a large chamber that was evenly lit by light from above.

The room was more than a hundred feet high and had to be forty or fifty feet wide. Above him were other levels of stone, the walls sweeping in and out like frozen waves, sometimes making the projecting rock narrow, sometimes wide, each seeming to be a separate floor surrounding the center of the cavern. From where Kattrick stood, it looked like a huge hole had been poked through the center of a multi-floored building, leaving each floor with a ragged hole in its center.

Far above, sunlight came through a long, narrow slit in the chamber's ceiling, filling the room with a soft, even glow.

At his feet, crystal-clear and perfectly still, was a pool of water.

The others went up the last steps and stood without saying a word. Even J.D., who usually kept up a constant string of swear words, jokes, insults, and useless talk, was stunned into silence.

Finally, walking around the pool, looking up at the slit in the ceiling, turning in a circle to see what stood around him, Kattrick thought out loud, trying to make sense of what he saw: "There must have been cracks on top of the mesa, cracks that went down into the center of the formation. A few thousand years of rain hollowed out the mesa from the inside, creating one floor, wearing through it, creating another floor, wearing through that, and so on for centuries."

He turned and pointed to the tunnel through which they had come.

"Finding a crack that led to the outside, the water carved it out like a drainpipe."

The others only stared, half listening to his theory, not much interested in the whats and whys. They had been brought along as labor, not big thinkers.

J.D. and Navajo Bob had been leading a preferred

life of loafing around the trading post back in Mexican Hat, doing odd jobs whenever their money ran out. But Kattrick, a fancy oil company geologist, had offered good money to anyone who could get the supplies, equip the boats, and take him down the river. The trip sounded like too much work, but the geologist offered to hire somebody else to do the hard stuff.

That sealed the deal, and J.D. and Bob had a good laugh on the way back from recruiting Little Jake. It would be a real adventure, they had told him. We'll help you with everything, they said.

Still amazed by the cavern, Kattrick found another set of steps that led upward from the rock floor where they had come out of the tunnel. Barely keeping his big boots in the rounded holes, he worked his way up ten or twelve feet and stepped out onto a level of rock much like the one below it. This level held another pool of water and led to another set of steps. He continued to climb to the next level and then the next. It confirmed his theory that cascading rain had carved out each of the levels as each burst of water sought out the drain.

It was remarkable, Kattrick thought. Remarkable!

Getting close to the slit in the ceiling, he continued up footholds that led to a shelf of rock circling the entire chamber. Leaning over and using his hands for balance, Kattrick stepped out of the last foothold and stood up.

His jaw dropped.

Along the back of the top shelf of rock, tucked

between the floor and the ceiling above, was a roughly flat wall covered with petroglyphs. Perhaps as high as eight feet in places, it must have been several hundred feet around in four distinct, continuous panels, each about fifty feet long.

Kattrick was looking at a vast array of symbols etched into the sandstone surface: corn, deer, antelope, men, hands, spirals, circles, arrows, rain, sun, snakes, spiders, scorpions. He had seen symbols like these at archaeological sites but never so many and never in any one place.

The space did not appear as if anyone had lived there, Kattrick thought, but that was no surprise. The Anasazi preferred open places for their homes, like the ruins built into the sides of cliffs. This place must have been special, maybe a holy place reserved for particular occasions or a repository for historical stories. Whatever their purpose, the panels of symbols were the largest he had ever seen or heard of.

Coming up behind him, J.D. whistled long and low.

"Man, would you look at this! Who would have thought the Anasazi would have ever found this place? Beats anything I ever saw." He walked over and ran his hands across the wall. Maybe seven hundred or eight hundred years had passed since someone scraped and chipped away at the figures, telling whatever story the symbols conveyed.

Moving along the panel, he glanced back. Little Jake had come up the steps and was behind him, but Bob had not moved an inch from the last foothold.

J.D. looked close and saw sweat covering his face. Bob was a Navajo. His people were historic enemies of the Anasazi, the Ancient Ones. If there was a story told by the rock figures, it was not told for him to hear. The quiver in Bob's cheeks betrayed his feelings: Enemy spirits might be here, right here, now, watching them. The *chindi* of the Ancient Ones, their spirits after death, might be guarding the rooms. It was not a place to be.

J.D. laughed at him and called him a coward.

Bob looked back at J.D., fully spooked and far too scared to be insulted or even angered. He didn't want to be here, didn't belong. He was an intruder. They were *all* intruders.

"You don't mess with the dead," Bob said under his breath.

As Bob refused to budge and the Boss Man seemed absorbed in what he was looking at, J.D. and Little Jake made a slow tour around the rock shelf. The slightly rounded wall carved out by the swirling waters coming through the slit was higher than their heads in most places, its surface smooth and even. J.D. noticed that pots on woven mats stood in several places under the panels. Stones for grinding corn leaned against the wall with other artifacts.

J.D. relit his lantern to look at the pots more closely.

Not great in number, they were palm-sized to maybe two feet tall and a foot or more in diameter, some with lids.

They would have been used to store small items—

corn, beans, seeds—or perhaps different colored sands, or maybe tools. Some of the pots had cracks, but most were as fine as the day they'd been made.

J.D. understood the significance immediately: He was looking at big money! If he could get these back to town, maybe haul a truckload to Flagstaff, he'd make a fortune selling them to collectors. Original and undisturbed?

Hardly even dirty? Maybe filled with the original grains?

He could name his price.

I'll be back later for them, he said to himself, whether it was part of the Boss Man's plans or not.

———

The rest of the day was spent moving equipment from the camp they'd made at the river into the chamber— hard, sweaty trips hauling gear up the different ledges of the cliff and through the tunnel to reestablish their camp around the bottom pool.

Kattrick ordered all traces of the previous night's camp wiped away and their tracks brushed out. He had the boats lifted out of the water and carried several yards back to where the brush hid them. He didn't think anyone else was on the river, but what he had found had to be guarded and protected. He didn't want his find discovered, and he certainly didn't intend to share it.

The following day, Kattrick created diagrams of the different levels of floors, the pools, the major rock

structures, the layers of sandstone, even the place-
ment of the wall drawings. Though driven by the
dream of the riches ahead, he was still a good geologist. Drawing what he could see let him imagine what
he could not see, and that was incredibly important.
The colored stones from the previous summer came
from somewhere, and if it was inside this chamber,
the drawings would show him where the sandstone
layers had been rammed together or squashed or
shifted.

As Kattrick worked on his drawings, J.D. and
Little Jake searched out more of the objects on the
floor, finding other pots, a dozen or so flint arrow-
heads, piles of old corn cobs, some grinding stones,
and more mats of woven yucca leaves.

Navajo Bob wasn't looking at all. He wanted
nothing to do with their exploring and still refused to
even step on the top floor, no matter how many
insults J.D. hurled at him.

In the afternoon, the light dimmed in the chamber
as dark bottoms of clouds passed over the slit in the
ceiling.

Distant thunder could be heard. After a few
minutes, drops of water made rings on the surface of
the pools. With little warning, the drops became
larger, and a solid cloud of spray and mist filled the
air as rain funneled through the slit above them, past
the top floor, and into the pools below. The four men
hunkered down and watched, their hands pressed
over their ears as the sound grew and echoed around
them. When the fury quit and a little sun shone again,

a rainbow appeared in the cavern's mist, draping the full length of the slit and filling the inside of the chamber with a glow of brilliant colors.

Another remarkable thing, Kattrick thought.

On the morning of the third day, Little Jake came to the bottom pool and brought Kattrick a medium-sized pottery jar he had found inside a larger storage pot, then went to look for more. Pouring the contents out on a blanket, Kattrick stared at what he saw.

Five or six large, green, glassy-looking stones, about thirty smaller red rocks, and several large chunks of polished blue stone laced with delicate streaks of what looked like gold. Mixed with the bigger pieces, a small crystal lay loose against the weave of the blanket.

Kattrick stared at it. His heart was pumping in his ears, and his throat was dry enough to crack as he carefully picked it up. He knew it was a diamond but opened his pocketknife and scraped the side to make sure. The blade left no mark.

His face ashen, he kept his composure even as his stomach turned somersaults. He hoped that the others hadn't noticed.

Carefully scooping the crystal and other stones back into the jar, Kattrick took a moment to calm himself. Forget the drawings—there had to be an opening. He struggled out a command.

"Jake! This is too many stones to just be from trading, they must have come from inside here someplace. Get J.D. There's gotta be an opening to a lava vent pipe. Everything we've seen so far is the result of time and water over sandstone, but these babies came out of a blow-hole, and somebody had to dig them out."

With Bob still not budging from his sitting place next to the tunnel they'd come through, the other three worked from the entrance tunnel in a clockwise direction, bottom to top, each man searching a section of the chamber.

As they covered every part of the cave, it wasn't long before a number of hidden openings were found. Some were just hollows in the wall, others went farther, leading down and under the main chamber.

There was a sudden shout. Following the voice to a narrow sliver of a crack, Kattrick dropped to his hands and knees and crawled through. Squeezing sideways past Little Jake, he slid into a smaller, much darker chamber.

The flickering light of his lantern refused to reflect from the dull, black walls. His eyes as big as quarters, he saw the sandstone of the passageway give way to a coarse, dense, dark rock.

Lava!

Kattrick scoured the small chamber as well as he could by the light of all the lanterns. Instead of erupting through the layers of sand and rock in the vast valley through which the San Juan River was destined to run, the gasses must have leaked off enough that the lava squeezed up but lost its momentum, then was too weak to break the surface.

Probably that was what had crushed the sandstone to make it wear away so easily from the center of the mesa, Kattrick thought—and probably the reason the river had circled this mesa in the first place, a random hard bump in the otherwise uniform layers of rock.

Stymied by not making it to the surface, the boiling hot lava from miles below had slowed, stopped, and cooled in place, forming a long bubble of the dark rock, full of debris scraped from the sides along the way. The deeper the source of the lava, the greater the pressure and heat, and the more likely that even more valuable gemstones had been carried along with the lava.

In the uneven light of the lanterns, Kattrick turned to Little Jake: "The Anasazi must have chipped away big chunks of this stuff and carried them up to the pools, where they broke them into smaller pieces. They kept the large stones for trading and jewelry-making and left the scrap.

"When it rained and the pools overflowed, all the throwaway rock washed out the tunnel and over the ledge."

Soon, the smoke from the lanterns and the stuffiness of the small cave became too much, and everyone returned to the entrance pool. The clouds were back overhead and the chamber was dark again. The thunder rumbled, and an occasional flash of lightning threw a momentary glow around them, warning of the storm brewing outside.

As the four sat around a blanket rolled out for their lunch, a loud crackle bounced across the walls. The chamber lit up with a flash, followed by a huge boom echoing from every direction. The four men cursed and shouted, covering their ears.

Struggling back to their knees, they froze in place as the sounds of the thunder were replaced by the rumbling of rocks. As fear twisted their stomachs, the crashing sounds slowly stopped.

Quickly on their feet, three men scrambled for the tunnel.

Everyone but Bob. Bob had rolled back into his sitting position, wide-eyed in terror. He had heard Coyote's laughter in the thunder and wouldn't move an inch.

You don't mess with the dead.

Kattrick made it to the tunnel first, dropped down, and shot through the narrow passageway. Within half a minute, he barreled back out, shoving the others out of the way and choking on the billowing, dust-laden air that followed him.

Lightning had hit the side of the mesa, shattering the massive rock bluffs into a landslide of broken rock and dirt, covering the outside entrance of the tunnel.

His body jerked back and forth as Kattrick struggled to breathe through the dust. Hacking, his lungs screaming, he rushed to the pool and submerged his head, then lifted it out and drank deep—anything to wash away the dust.

More puffs belched out of the tunnel opening, and then all was silent. Panic slowly gave way to despair as the men looked into each other's eyes.

They were trapped.

CHAPTER 2

MEXICAN HAT, UTAH, TODAY

Reaching with the broom as far as he could under the large platforms, Mogi Franklin pulled piles of sand, dirt, dried mud, and dust to the center of the aisle. Frank Tsosie used the grain shovel as a dustpan, and the piles were swept up and dumped into the big trashcan next to the door. It was hard enough work, and Mogi wasn't enthused that he and Frank were the only ones sweeping the floor of a building the size of a small aircraft hangar.

It wasn't what he liked to do with his Saturdays, but today was different.

Mogi was fourteen and tall for his age, but his muscles had not yet caught up with his bones, and so he was gangly and spindly and a little awkward, which is to say, normal for where he was in life. He took after his mom's side of the family in what he looked like and his shyness but seemed to be a sum of both families on the brain side: He was smart, quick-minded, mentally disciplined, and orderly, and had natural talents for solving problems. Because of this, he was a year ahead at Bluff High School and had been invited to help with the work.

Pushing the broom along the back wall, he glanced up to the ceiling. Suspended from the curving rafters twenty feet above hung a strange-looking wooden boat. Instead of curving sides that met underneath to form a keel, like an ordinary rowboat, the sides were almost straight up and down, with overlapping boards like the sides of a house.

Meeting the bottom of the sides all around in sweeping curves, a flat floor made the inside of the boat two or maybe even three feet deep. Across the top, it had been enclosed by a curved deck on each end, with latching doors that must have led to storage compartments. There was an opening in the center for whoever rowed the boat.

Something bad had happened to it. The floor was smashed and broken close to the front, and a large hole poked through the wooden slats running from the bottom up to a splintered rim.

"Mr. Bottington," Mogi called up front to a large man directing other teenagers. "What's that?"

Burl Bottington was the owner of San Juan River Expeditions, a wilderness rafting company in the village of Mexican Hat, about twenty miles west of where Mogi lived in Bluff. A big, burly man with huge arms, chest, and neck, matched by a sizable stomach, which confirmed that he never let the word *diet* into his lifestyle. He was always laughing and joking and had a story for every occasion. Everyone was his friend, and he was a special favorite of Bluff students.

Burl looked up at the boat and smiled.

"Well, now, that there's a real San Juan River mystery. Let's get some of the cleanin' started and I'll tell you about some disappearing people and ghosts. You don't mind hearin' about disappearing people and ghosts, do ya?"

"No, sir, I'd like that," Mogi answered.

"We haven't already started cleaning?" Frank asked Mogi as Mr. Bottington rejoined the teenagers outside.

"He must be talking about the stuff outside," Mogi replied. "But this is my first time. Jennifer's been through this before. She said the building had to be cleaned before any of the outside stuff can be put back in and handed me the broom."

"How does this work again?" Frank asked.

"It's a deal with the high school," Mogi answered.

"Mr. Bottington'll take a hundred groups of people or so down the San Juan on rafts this summer. At the end of the season in the fall, he throws everything in here and takes a vacation. The last weekend of March the next year—which is today—the school sends over a bunch of volunteers to get everything out of the building, clean things up, repair anything that needs repairing, and put it all back in, nice and neat.

"In return, Mr. Bottington gives the school a free raft trip for students who want to go down the river during the April school break. When we get back, we'll clean what we used, and then he's ready for the paying customers. Have you ever been rafting before?"

"Nope."

"Are there even rivers where you live?"

Frank smiled. "There's not even water where I live. Our grandparents' hogan is about ten miles from the highway in the Lukachukai Mountains, maybe a hundred miles from here. Running water, to us, is the stuff in the bottom of a gulley during a rainstorm. We even have to haul our drinking water in the back of a pickup."

Mogi couldn't quite imagine it. Frank and his twin sister, Becky, were Navajo Indians from the reservation. They and their dad had come to Bluff from Arizona after Christmas, living in Bluff while he worked on a drilling crew out of Aneth, a tiny town surrounded by gas wells thirty minutes east of Bluff.

"You miss home?" Mogi asked.

"Not really. My mom stayed to help my grandparents, so we go back on weekends to help with the sheep. We live in a trailer house on the same property.

"My dad is a jeweler, a really good one, but the price of turquoise is really high, and he can't sell enough jewelry to cover the cost, so he took a job off the reservation. Everybody we know is in the same shape—leaving their homes to find work. It's bad times. It's hard for jewelers to even find good turquoise, much less all they need to make a good business."

"Isn't turquoise kind of important in your culture?"

"Yeah. Turquoise means a lot to the Navajo people. It's wrapped up in our spirit. It's one of the things that makes our jewelry special and helps make the ceremonies right."

"You guys finished yet?" His sister Jennifer asked, coming in from outside with Becky. Jennifer was seventeen, three years older than Mogi. Frank and Becky, who were in some of his classes, were fifteen.

"Jennifer!" Mr. Bottington called. "Show your brother how to wash the rescue ropes."

Jennifer definitely took after her father. Shorter than Mogi by half a foot, with thick, brown hair cut short, she was strong, athletic, and graceful. Whereas her brother was the obsessive, analytical, adventurous problem-solver, Jennifer was mature beyond her years, a cautious, emotionally centered people-person. He pushed her to do more than she thought she ought to, she pulled him back into what was reasonable.

Both of them had great Franklin family smiles.

Jennifer led Mogi, Frank, and Becky to an inside wall with a large array of pegs. She took gallon-sized canvas bags off the pegs until her arms were full and dumped them into a pile at a utility sink next to the door. She pulled a rope out of one of the bags, turned on the faucet, and fed the rope into the sink under the running water as she ran her hands over the alternating red and white threads.

"The idea is to get enough of the mud and yuck off that you can see the color," she said.

Frank and Becky each grabbed a bag and did the best they could to follow Jennifer's example.

"You wash, and I'll lay them out to dry," Mogi said as he gathered the first pile of wet ropes and went outside.

Deciding against stringing them across the parking lot where students were milling about, he laid each rope out in a spiral. Carefully playing it through his fingers, he tried to make each new loop a half-inch from the previous one, sometimes using a fingertip to get the spacing just right.

"What are you doing?" Becky had brought another rope and was watching Mogi.

"Well, hey, you know. Don't want it to look bad while it's drying."

"You gotta watch out for dork-boy here," Jennifer said as she came up to join them. "He has strange and mysterious ways."

Earlier that morning, the students had pulled all the equipment out of the storage building and spread it over the parking lot. There were piles of river bags, tents, rafts, raft frames, oars, paddles, pumps, hundreds of nylon straps, rainsuits, personal flotation devices, stoves, pots and pans, grills, rain flies, air pumps, folding chairs, folding tables, more ropes, and some things Mogi didn't recognize.

Mr. Bottington ran hoses from the outside faucets to the different piles, making jokes as students sprayed the equipment and themselves. Once washed, everything was laid out in the parking lot to dry. Stuff not to be cleaned with water, like stoves, lanterns, and pumps, were moved to a couple of tables to be wiped off, lubricated when needed, and set aside.

Everyone was busy, and the Bottington House of Rafting took on the appearance of a beehive. The San Juan Expeditions building and parking lot sat a hundred feet off the main—and only—street through Mexican Hat, about a half-mile from the raft launch point on the San Juan River.

Starting in the high mountains of southern Colorado, then flowing mostly west across the top of New Mexico, the San Juan River passed within a couple of miles of the aptly named *Four Corners*, where the two states also met Arizona and Utah, then continued straight west through Utah until it ran into Lake Powell. One of the premier wilderness rivers in the Southwest, it was famous for its deep, narrow, twisting canyons.

As Mogi finished laying out the last of the rescue ropes, Mr. Bottington called everyone over to a cooler of drinks just inside the door. Teenagers streamed in with some of the folding chairs, grabbed cans of soda, and spread out around the large man.

Smiling as he looked up at the damaged boat hanging from the ceiling, Burl drew up a small folding chair and maneuvered his large body into it, making the teenagers fear for its survival.

"Well, now, if all of you will die-rect your eyes there in the back, there's an old boat hangin' from the ceilin' that's been banged up a little. Right up there is a gen-u-wine San Juan River mystery."

Burl pulled another chair around, propped his feet against the leg bar, pushed his glasses up on his nose, and leaned back with his hands behind his head.

"That boat belonged to ol' Norm Nevills hisself. It got smashed up a long time ago, long time before I ever showed up. Norm built that boat from raw lumber to take people on river trips before there were any commercial outfits around here. He worked on the design for a long time to get it where it would carry the people and all the equipment and handle all the rapids, way before they started using these fancy inflatable jobbies. Ol' Norm's the guy who started the expedition business on the San Juan, back in '36."

Burl looked over the young faces listening to him.

"Y'all ever heard of the ghosts of the San Juan?"

No one answered back, but several grinned at each other. It was going to be another tall tale from Burl the Storyteller.

Mr. Bottington shifted his bottom in the chair and scratched his mostly bald head.

"Well, it was back in 1934 that one of the locals paid ol' Norm fifty buckaroos to borrow a couple of his boats. Norm hadn't started any kind of business yet and didn't have much equipment, but fifty bucks was a goodly sum in those days, and he let 'im have the best two boats he had. It was in April and had been one of those real rainy springs like we don't have but every hundred years or so, so the river was running real high.

"Anyway, two days later, four men were seen loading the two boats with all sorts of stuff. Piles of tarps, blankets, food, shovels, picks, campin' equipment, water pouches, and a bunch of other stuff had been laid out on the bank of the river and then stuffed into the boat's compartments.

"They left in the two boats about noon and were never seen again."

Burl shifted in his chair and pointed to the hulk of a boat in the air.

"That boat was found about a week after they left, stuck on a sandbar on the other side of Steer Gulch. Some Indian kids found it, and the word finally got back to Norm. He took another boat and went down the river, lookin' all around as he went.

"When he found that boat there, battered and broken up, completely empty, with no equipment in it, he stretched a big tarp over the whole bottom of the boat, makin' it so it would float in the water again, and towed it down to Clay Hills Crossin' where Doris picked 'im up.

"Doris was his wife, ya know, and the two of 'em started offering regular trips down the river two years later, the very first commercial trips in this part of the country, even before anybody was doing the Colorado through the Grand Canyon. Well, anyway, Norm said that he never saw anythin' along the river, no camp or anythin'. No signs along the bank, no fire rings, no disturbed camping spots—nothin'. Those four guys just up and vanished."

"Why did they go down the river in the first place?" one of the teenagers asked.

"Well, nobody knew for sure, you understand, but one of the men turned out to be a geologist who had been on the river the year before, doin' surveys for some oil company.

"This trip, though, didn't have anythin' to do with the oil company, 'cause nobody at any of the oil companies knew anythin' about it. A rumor got started that the geologist had discovered gold the year before and was tryin' to get back to it. I kind of doubt it, though, 'cause nobody's ever found enough gold worth sweatin' over on this whole river."

Burl stopped to take a breath.

"They didn't find any bodies?" Mogi asked.

"Not a one. No skin, no bones, no clothes, no nothin'. Never found the other boat, either. They couldn't even find signs along the banks where they might have camped. Some people thought the men must have hiked out south through the reservation, but no Indian ever saw 'em, which would typically have been the case. They might have floated way down the river in the other boat, but nobody in the settlements downstream ever saw anybody either.

"It was decided that they up and died along the river, the devil buryin' their bodies someplace and their ghosts just floatin' around the canyon walls unto this very day. It was them ghosts that took the boats on down the river, leavin' one of them behind just to make fun of us.

"It's been many a time on the river that I've heard whisperin' voices and cryin' in the night when there's been nobody there, and I'm pretty sure it's them ghosts who can't find their eternal rest, and I'm not lyin' to ya!" Burl added, grinning in an I-just-lied-to-you way.

With a grunt, he finished off his drink with a long slurp, stood up, called for the others to get to it, and went for an extension cord to run the air pump.

Four men, two boats, outfitted for a trip, Mogi said to himself. And not one comes back. No bodies, no camp, no equipment, no tracks, and one of them was even a geologist who had been on the river before.

Still thinking about it, he headed over to the other teens as the big, sixteen-foot whitewater rafts were starting to balloon up under the force of the air pump. It took almost an hour to inflate all the rafts and then an hour more to go over them with soapy water. Any leaks in a raft made the soap bubble and were circled with a marker. Mr. Bottington would add a patch later.

As the rafts dried, the flow of equipment started back into the building, which actually had been an aircraft hangar before it was taken down and moved to Mexican Hat. Around twenty feet tall, it was made of half-circles of metal struts covered with wavy tin panels for the roof, with two tall, rectangular doors hung on a long rail across the front opening.

In the center, the big, wooden platforms Mogi had swept under held the deflated rafts off the floor and kept the cold cement from damaging the fabric.

Next to a small office on the left, shelves made out of two-by-fours and plywood reached the ceiling and held the camping equipment. Along the right side, latticework shelving held the large air pumps, tents, poles, paddles, and other long equipment.

The rafting frames were made of aluminum pipe and put together so they sat across the rafts. Each set was propped up along the back wall. The ten-foot oars were stacked in a corner, and large racks next to them held the two hundred or so straps used to tie everything to the rafts.

Mogi and Frank lowered long poles from the ceiling to skewer the PFDs and then pulled them back up so they were suspended above the other equipment. The rainsuits were put on hangers, hung on a pole, and lofted up next to the PFDs. Beneath translucent panels in the roof, the different blues, greens, reds, yellows, and oranges formed a carpet of color against the drab ceiling.

Tents were rolled up, stored in their bags, and stacked neatly in the latticework. Ropes were hung from pegs. The large waterproof dry bags where passengers stored their personal gear were laid into wooden bins—grouped by color, thanks to Mogi—the camping equipment was gathered and sorted into the shelves, and chairs folded and stored. As a last gasp of organization, anything that was left over was hung from pegs next to the door.

In the fading light of dusk, most of the teenagers waved their goodbyes and headed for their cars. Mogi continued counting everything and making a list of the equipment for Mr. Bottington.

"The boy's in heaven," Jennifer said to Frank and Becky as they sat around a table with Mr. Bottington, waiting. "If we don't do something, he'll be counting the cracks in the cement. I suspect one of my parents accidentally dropped him on his head as a child, but they've never confessed. I just hope he doesn't notice the filing cabinet in your office."

Burl Bottington laughed and grinned. "The boy's special, ain't he? I do appreciate 'im, though. I'm not sure I've ever had a count of the stuff I have. As for the filin' cabinet, it might take the whole summer, even for somebody with a gift.

"Yo! Hey, son!" the jovial man called, interrupting Mogi as he stopped to sort the water jugs by size, large on the left. "I was happenin' to remember how good the ice cream is up at the Dairy Queen. Why don't you and your friends meet me up yonder and we'll do a quality check?" He roared with laughter.

Mogi smiled. It must have dropped thirty degrees when the sun went down, but Mr. Bottington was not one to pass on an opportunity to have a little dessert before supper.

CHAPTER 3

"Everybody listen up!" Mogi turned as Mr. Jennings balanced on a raft's front tube and shouted over the noisy crowd.

It was an April afternoon on the San Juan River outside the town limits of Bluff, twenty miles or so upriver from Mexican Hat. The noise slowly subsided, and Mr. Jennings waited a number of seconds before speaking.

"Make sure you've got your school cameras and they're in your waterproof boxes, and those boxes are securely strapped onto the safety lines on top of the tubes. I do not—I repeat, do *not*—want to lose a camera like we did last year. If you have your own cameras, make sure they're protected as well."

Mr. Jennings was Bluff High School's geology teacher, and, as the teacher-in-charge for this year's rafting trip, not surprisingly made its theme the mapping of the river canyon's different layers of rock, from one end to the other.

"Remember, this is not a vacation," he said. "You will have fun, but you will also be expected to do a little work. We can't waste this opportunity to do a little geology."

This brought groans and sighs from the group.

"We'll be stopping every half-mile to photograph both sides of the canyon. Those of you with cameras, make sure you write down the GPS coordinates at the place you take a picture.

"Those of you with rock hammers will be gathering rocks and bagging them as we go along. You also will be responsible for labeling the bags with the GPS locations. When we get back, we'll build a panorama of the whole canyon. Everybody's thinking *work*, right?"

The responses were muddled, but they were enough for him. Clicking the last buckle on his PFD, Mr. Jennings found an empty space on the front tube and just managed to sit down as the raft was shoved off from the bank, hurried on by screams and hoots of laughter as the other boats followed.

An oarsman sitting in the center of each raft used two long oars to guide the boat into the current. Mr. Bottington had hired and trained many of the older high school students in the area, employing the young men and women during the summer to row his rafts. Three of them had been hired for the school's spring break raft trip, and two Bluff High teachers shared the rowing duties as well.

The passengers sat on ice chests or the tubes of the

raft, sometimes straddling them to drag their feet in the water.

In the last raft to leave, Burl Bottington pulled on his oars with long, patient strokes. His boat had no passengers, which gave him plenty of room to carry the waterproof bags of clothing, camping equipment, water, and food. Each of the other rafts carried one ice chest, Mr. Bottington's had three.

As always, he pulled slow and steady, perfectly in tune with the river, perfectly positioned in the current. He loved the river, could feel its muddy current through his bones, could feel the spirit as it drew the rafts along. Once away from the shore, things that seemed important on land fell into a more proper perspective, and the river itself took on the role of commander-in-chief.

———

"This is harder than I expected."

Jennifer laughed at her brother. "You wimp. Last year, Mrs. Harrington, the biology teacher, was in charge. We'd stop and gather flowers, then stop and gather grasses, then stop and catch bugs. Drove me nuts!"

Becky laughed. Frank was behind Mogi on the left side of the raft while Becky was behind Jennifer on the right.

There wasn't much to do until they pulled into shore, and then it seemed like a madhouse with people taking pictures, others whacking rocks with hammers, everyone screaming to find out the GPS coordinates, and then a fevered push to borrow markers to write on plastic bags as they all got back into the rafts.

"Your dad liking his job?" Mogi asked as the raft drifted through a wide valley surrounded by distant cliffs.

"It's all right," Frank answered. "He misses being on his own. But what he really hates is that drilling work is tough on his hands. He can't do the really fine stamp-work on silver when his fingers get callused."

"Mogi," Becky asked, "have you found out anything more about your ghosts?"

"There was a book in the library with stories about mysteries and secrets in Utah, but it had the same information Mr. Bottington gave," he said. "I found a couple of newspaper articles on the web talking about the mystery because it's never been solved, and one reference to a book, but it was about the history of oil discovery in Utah and only had a couple of sentences about the oil company exploring the canyons."

"You think we'll see any ghosts?" Frank asked.

"I'd be happy if we could find bones, or maybe the other boat," Mogi said.

"Oh, sure," Jennifer said. "After only a million people floating this river over the last seven or eight decades, I bet we'll just stumble on something that they all missed."

"Stranger things have happened," Mogi said with a

head tilted toward his sister. "This is spooky country, full of spirits. Don't forget about all the Anasazi ruins around this place—they're probably full of ghosts flying around."

"Navajo believe that ruins of the Ancient Ones still hold some of the spirits of the dead," Becky said. "But I'm not sure they fly around. You usually only get messed with if you're inside the ruin."

"I'll take a ruin full of ghosts over skinwalkers," Frank said. "*Yenaldooshi*—that's what we call skinwalkers. Skinwalkers are people who can turn into animals, like wolves, or coyotes, or even ravens. They follow you around. We know an old lady over on a mesa south of our hogan who's a skinwalker."

Frank continued telling stories—what skinwalkers looked like, the animals they could change into, and a few instances in which their curses had killed people. Mogi was polite but not very believing. He hadn't known the Navajo honestly believed in spirits that inhabited real people and could walk around through everyday life.

None of it seemed very reasonable to him.

After a few hours, the rafts came to a bend of the river with a grove of tall cottonwood trees. Eager to get away from the awkward, slow-moving boats, their passengers hardly waited to pull into the sandy shore before jumping off into the water and wading onto the beach, splashing each other, or chasing each other through the trees.

Mr. Bottington pulled in, and what teenagers

could be found formed a line to move the equipment from his raft to the camping spot. He chose a spot for the kitchen box, but the heavy ice chests were left in the rafts, food would be taken out as needed.

Tents were soon rolled out and erected, sleeping pads and bags laid inside, waterproof bags opened and emptied as people changed into warmer clothes. Mr. Bottington and the two teachers set up the kitchen under a large plastic tarp strung among the trees. Narrow folding tables were set out, stands unfolded for the stoves, lanterns hung from the trees, and a fire was lit. A large grill was positioned over the flames, and the smell of charbroiled hamburgers was soon drifting through camp.

———

The next morning, doing everything in reverse and finally strapping down all the equipment, the teenagers gathered around Mr. Jennings, ready for the second day.

"In a couple of hours," he said, "we're going to pull over and tie up. We're all going for a hike. We're going to see a vent pipe."

A hike would be good, Mogi thought. Riding the whole day without breaks except to work was boring, even if the scenery was great. He was ready to *do* something.

"About thirty million years ago," Mr. Jennings continued, "there was an eruption that left an unusual geologic feature, called a vent pipe, a few miles down-river from here.

"You all know about the crust and mantle of the earth, right?" The students agreed with a nod of their heads.

"Imagine a bunch of gasses at a point where the crust meets the mantle. For some reason, those gasses explode and shoot up through the crust, with hot lava following behind.

"When the gasses break the surface, they blow out a mixture of all sorts of rocks that they scraped from the sides of the hole along the way—from the mantle, from the lower surface of the crust, from all of the layers of rock that make up the crust, and from rocks in the top layer of the surface.

"The explosion spurts everything out like a bad pimple. The rocks that didn't blow into the country-side fall back into the hole and mix with the lava that's bubbling up. After everything settles down and cools, what you get is this tall, solid, roughly circular column of lava containing lots of different kinds of rock.

"In particular," he continued, getting warmed up as if he were back in the classroom, "it can contain precious or semi-precious gemstones that were formed under the extreme temperatures and pressures five to six miles below the crust. Sometimes, the gasses will also suck up some of the muck from deeper in the mantle, which can contain even more valuable types of gemstones.

"So if you want to do serious rock hunting, a vent

pipe is a great place to go. And just to pique your interest, the pipe that you're going to see today has the same features as the famous diamond mines of South Africa. Vent pipes were responsible for bringing diamonds to the surface."

"Have there ever been any diamonds found around here?" Mogi asked.

"Not that I know of. Most people wouldn't know a raw diamond if they saw it, though. It looks just like a piece of quartz. They'd probably throw it away. Other gemstones have been found, like red garnets. They're not very big, but they're valuable and make nice jewelry.

"Does anybody have any questions? Once we pull off and start the hike, everybody make sure you've got your water and your sunscreen," he called as the teenagers scattered to their rafts. The boats soon were off, flowing into the current and pushing their cargo through the clean, rich-smelling morning air.

The river, wide and shallow, moved back and forth across a valley lush with green bushes and grasses, set off by more of the giant cottonwood trees. Mogi imagined having to stop and pick flowers every time Mrs. Harrington saw a different one and decided that maybe gathering rocks wasn't so bad.

Less than an hour later, the rafts pulled onto a sandy beach on the left bank. Following one after another, the students thinned into a long line that looked like a centipede as it snaked itself up a series of narrow paths, angled through the hills, and moved onto a higher level of land overlooking the river valley.

Once they were there, the explorers saw a large hill of dark-colored rock in the distance, the well-eroded top of the vent pipe. Soon, the canyon echoed with the sounds of rock hammers whacking away pieces of geologic history.

CHAPTER 4

The visit to the vent pipe took the rest of the morning. When the rock hounds returned to the boats, they found Mr. Bottington laying out a lunch buffet on the folding tables. Spent from the hard work of pounding rock all morning, the students fell on the food like starving vultures, and there was a flurry of sandwich-making as they crowded around the tables. Clouds were building on the horizon, so the remnants of lunch were packed back in the coolers quickly, and the rafts pushed into the speeding current.

As the rafts drifted, Mogi turned and closely watched Mr. Bottington pull on the big oars of the supply raft. He appeared unhurried but efficient, smoothly reaching forward to place the black blades of the long, yellow oars into the water and then pulling in full strokes, his huge arms and shoulders directing the heavily laden boat downriver as it meandered in the current.

Mogi was fascinated with Mr. Bottington's coordination and strength, much like a dance, and imagined being in the seat, pulling and pushing the oars with the same skill. He wondered how well he could do the dance.

The rest of the day followed the pattern of the previous one—stopping, photographing, gathering, labeling, storing, starting again. Just after mid-afternoon, mushrooming thunderheads darkened the canyon and let loose a frenzy of water, rushing everyone into their rain jackets and pants. Though this kept the teenagers mostly dry, a rising wind whipped the rain into their faces, causing most of them to hunker down for protection.

The gusts blew the rafts back and forth across the river, and several bumped rocks along the shore or ran aground on sandbars.

Gradually, the thunderstorm passed.

As the students struggled into the day's campsite, slipping and sliding in the grease-like mud of the shore, the chores of unloading the boats became a mess, putting up tents became a mess, eating supper was a mess, and any planned activities for the evening died before they were ever begun. Mercifully, the day was soon declared officially over, and most people scrambled back to the tents to change clothes and play cards.

After heating a large pot of water for late-evening coffee and hot chocolate, Mr. Bottington was dishing out hot water for all who wanted it when Mogi made his way under the kitchen tarp and found Mr. Jennings sipping a cup of tea.

"Mr. Jennings, have you ever heard of the ghosts of the San Juan?"

The teacher glanced at Mr. Bottington after hearing a little laugh from the boatman.

"Sure, although I seem to have missed them every time I've gone down the river."

"Uh, do you know anything more about the story?" Mogi asked.

"Well, it is the most repeated ghost story on this river, I believe, but I may know a few details that most people don't, being as the lead man was a geologist. He was also a science professor at what's now Northern Arizona University in Flagstaff. He worked for oil companies during the summer to earn money on the side. Let's see...his name...was..." Mr. Jennings paused as he tried to remember, "Kattrick, Gordon Kattrick. Kattrick had gone down the San Juan the summer before, in 1933, on a mapping expedition for the Shell Oil Company.

"He came back by himself the next spring, in 1934, and hired three local men to outfit and manage two boats he rented. The rumor was that he'd found gold or gas or oil or something and kept it a secret from the company. I think he rented the boats from Nevills, didn't he?" Mr. Jennings asked the old river guide next to him, who nodded.

"Well, they went down the river," Mr. Jennings said, "and were never seen again. After the one wrecked boat was found, the university sent up an investigator to work with the local sheriff and the state police. Along with the others, he couldn't find any reason Kattrick would have gone down the river to begin with, so the rumors kept growing.

"There was only one unusual thing," Mr. Jennings said, "but it didn't show up until later. The university sent their investigator to Shell's field office to review the report of what had been found the year before. They were pretty interested in any truth to there being gold, as you might imagine.

"And it wouldn't have been any surprise if Kattrick had found something and not reported it. Apparently, he was not a pleasant person to get along with. The investigator went back into the papers of the '33 expedition and found something that was a little extraordinary."

Mogi's ears perked up. "What?"

"Well, Shell had done two or three rock surveys in the canyon, dating back a few years. They continued to do surveys because the science of oil exploration was just beginning and they were always changing their theories about what different rock formations meant. As a matter of policy, they gathered rocks during each trip and compared them to previous trips. In every case, what they found was more or less what they had always found.

"The 1933 expedition, however, had brought back one bag of samples that didn't match the previous surveys. It was a lot of green glass and red garnets gathered from the vent pipe that we were at this morning."

"What's green glass?"

"Green glass is a name for a rock that's special to gaseous eruptions. It's got all sorts of oddball elements in it.

"Anyway, these elements get mixed together, oh, say, five or six miles below the surface of the earth where there's a lot of pressure and heat, and they make a rock that's green and glassy-looking. It's rare and pretty valuable but isn't unknown around volcanoes or vent pipes. Why those types of rocks hadn't shown up before was considered just luck on Kattrick's part."

"How do you know all this stuff?" Mogi asked.

"I was actually a brilliant geologist before I became a school teacher," Mr. Jennings said, which brought another little laugh from the big man standing next to him.

CHAPTER 5

The night was cold, and Jennifer was happy to snuggle deep into her thick sleeping bag. She asked Becky, who was sharing her tent, about life on the reservation.

"My dad was taught to be a silversmith by his father and his grandfather and learned to work with gemstones from my uncle," Becky said. "By combining silver and stones, he's created a lot of jewelry. He's even won First Place at a state fair. Anyway, he loves making jewelry and had been earning enough money to make a living until the price of good turquoise went too high. That's why he's working on the drilling rig. We didn't have enough money to buy feed for the winter."

"What's your mom doing?"

"She stayed with the house, taking care of my grandparents. My grandmother doesn't speak English and wouldn't leave the hogan, so my mom decided it wasn't worth it to force her to leave. We drive back on the weekends to take supplies and work the sheep."

"Is your hogan made out of mud and stuff? Isn't that the traditional way of making them?"

Becky laughed. "You need to come visit us sometime.

"You might think that a hogan is a mud hut or something, but it's not bad at all. We have two hogans, one built by my great-grandfather, but it's fallen down and not used anymore. The other one is where my grandparents live.

"Frank and I and our family live in a house trailer that's on the same property.

"My grandmother is a very, very neat person, so her hogan is very clean and orderly. The floor is dirt, but every square inch is covered by a rug or blanket. I spent a lot of my time growing up using a rug beater."

Becky bunched up the pillow and lay back on her sleeping bag, pulling her jacket up around her.

"What I miss most is the country. There's something that happens to you, you know, when you live in contact with everything. The hogan is made of logs and mud, so when I'm in it, I'm lying on the ground, surrounded by the earth, and when I take the sheep out to graze, there's the land all around me. When we harvest our corn and beans, we get the ground all over us." She rolled over and rested her head in the crook of her arm.

"I don't mean we're dirty. I mean that we're, like, part of the earth. We're connected to it. We're aware of the ground, of the sky, of the sun and the moon, the stars and clouds. We're really in tune with things. I haven't gotten used to living in the city."

Jennifer smiled. Calling Bluff a city wasn't something she heard very often.

"Can I ask you a question?" Becky said.

"Sure," Jennifer replied, propping herself up on an elbow.

"Where'd your brother get his name? I mean, his name's not really *Mogi*, right?"

Jennifer laughed. "Well, yeah, it's only a nickname. Nobody has ever called him by his real name, Nathaniel. Okay, so you know the Moki Dugway that's on Highway 261? That's the twisty, curvy part of the road that goes straight up the cliffs north of Mexican Hat?"

"Yeah, I think so."

"Well, when my brother was little, whenever we went up or down that road, instead of being scared, he'd just laugh and laugh and laugh. So we started calling him *Moki*. But he couldn't say a *k*, so when he said *Moki*, it always sounded like *Mogi*. So that's what we called him. He still laughs whenever we're on it."

"So, a kid named after a highway," Becky said. "You know that's kind of goofy, right?"

Jennifer giggled as she drifted off to sleep.

———

During the morning gathering, Mr. Jennings pointed on the map.

"We're coming to the Goosenecks. The river

makes big loops, going in one direction and then looping back on itself to where it's only a few hundred feet from where it was a couple of miles before but with a stretch of land between the two points. That land is called the neck of the gooseneck.

"We're going to camp tonight where the neck area got so thin on one gooseneck that it collapsed. The river stopped going around the loop and started flowing right through the neck area, eventually wearing it away completely. This left a mesa all by itself, south of the river, completely disconnected to anything around it, which makes it completely on the Navajo reservation.

"Chances are high that when we look at a stranded mesa, no human has ever set foot on top of it.

"You'll also see when we get there how much the cliffs have eroded away, so the sides of the canyon are now a series of ledges. Some of the boulders we have to go around in the river were once part of the cliffs high overhead."

The rafts continued gliding in the current, sweeping around one loop after another. Mogi's neck hurt from looking up so much. It must be a couple of thousand feet to the rim, he thought. We must look like ants on donuts.

It was mid-afternoon when the rafts pulled into a wide beach on the outside of a bend in the river. The plan was to make camp fifty feet up a wide draw.

"This is the stranded mesa I told you about," Mr. Jennings said. "If anybody's interested in a hike, you can take off up this draw, walk a couple of miles, and come out another draw a hundred yards down the river. But it's really the same draw. But before you go, I see some clouds on the horizon, so everyone needs to get their tents up sooner rather than later."

A long line of teenagers formed again to unload the rafts. After Mogi and Frank had gotten their stuff and put up their tent, they decided to take the hike Mr. Jennings had mentioned.

"We're going to try to make it around the mesa before we eat," Mogi called to his sister as he and Frank shouldered their daypacks. He had brought his good camera with its big lens from home. He draped the strap over his shoulder as they took off up the sandy draw.

Mogi had expected the hike to be easy since the draw had once been the bottom of the river, but it was anything but smooth. Lots of boulders, patches of deep sand, and several areas of basketball-sized rocks made the walking difficult. And then there were the immense patches of cactus.

The two boys made it up the draw about half a mile before the clouds that had seemed so distant were suddenly over them and began to sprinkle.

"We'd better get out of the bottom in case a flash flood comes," Mogi said as he scrambled up the side of the draw. "Did you bring your rainsuit?"

Frank hustled behind him. "Rainsuit? It was bright sunshine when we left. Did you bring yours?"

Mogi laughed. "Of course not. It was bright sunshine when we left."

The sky quickly grew dark. A few large drops

came randomly at first, then slow and steady, then fast. Soon, water gushed from above as if a faucet had been turned on.

"Head for that rock!" Mogi yelled as he yanked his jacket out of his pack and wrapped it around his camera.

The two boys crowded next to a house-sized boulder about fifty feet up the sloping side of the draw, across from the stranded mesa.

Thunder boomed and the wind increased as it whipped around them. The raindrops turned huge, whacking the boys like little bombs.

———

Back at camp, the sudden cloudburst had everyone scrambling to finish getting their rainflies hooked onto their tents and their equipment inside.

With their fly already on and secured, Jennifer was outside the tent, passing sleeping bags, packs, pillows, and bags of clothing inside to Becky. The huge raindrops surprised her, pounding on her back like exploding water balloons.

She hurriedly closed the dry bags and crawled into the tent, not realizing her knees were accidentally pressing the door's threshold into the sand to make a channel, sending a newborn river of rainwater directly inside.

"Aaaaaaiiiiiiihhhhhhh!" Jennifer screamed as she realized what was going on. Becky was pulling the sleeping bags and clothes into a large mass as far away as she could from the rapidly developing in-tent Jacuzzi. It was a much tougher task because she was laughing so hard both at the water coming in and at Jennifer, who looked like a wet cat.

———

Squeezed next to the big rock, Mogi and Frank were drenched. With the wind and the size of the raindrops, nothing was staying dry. Holding their packs on top of their heads—Mogi with his camera wrapped underneath him—it was all they could do to hunker down and wait out the storm.

"This is what we call a male rain," Frank said, grinning.

"Big, hard, fast, and angry, like a father. We call gentle rains female rains, mother rains that come slowly and quietly."

As the torrent subsided and a drizzle, then a mist, took its place, the two boys finally stood up and shook the puddles from their packs.

"Wow. Look at that," Mogi said.

The canyon and mesa had been transformed. Every ledge along the canyon walls, every stair step reaching toward the top of the mesas, every edge where a vertical face of rock had a low spot, now spouted a waterfall.

Big falls, small falls, single stream falls shooting their rushing water far out over rock ledges, broad falls that poured over rock sides like the curtain of rain off the edge of a roof. The waterfall directly across from them was huge.

The clouds continued to move up-canyon, letting the sun peek under the backside of the thunderhead, splashing bright light on the far cliffs downriver. Reflecting off the bottom of the clouds above Mogi, a golden glow filtered through the light rain, making the waterfalls glisten and shine.

Every surface of smooth rock shone wet, as if it were newly waxed. The drizzle and mist were thick as it caught the glow and turned the light into a brilliant rainbow above the camp and river Mogi could see in the distance.

Fading sunshine illuminated the dark billows of the underside of the thunderhead moving into the distance, highlighting the cloud with shades of yellow and auburn.

Shaking water from his jacket, Mogi quickly unwrapped his camera. He took several shots and a couple of panoramas across the width of the canyons and river. The lighting of the sun, the silver of the spilling water, the yellows and greens of the tents below him, the bright blue of the kitchen tarp in the distance, the reds and yellows of the rafts on the river, the burnished gold of the wet sandstone cliffs set off by the black of the desert varnish, the strong colors of the rainbow—surrounded by all this, Mogi found himself holding the button down as his camera clicked away.

Frank stood behind him, eyes closed, arms

extended with his palms out, taking slow, deep breaths.

Finished with his picture-taking, Mogi turned to look at him. Must be a Navajo thing, he thought. The moment was gone in less than a minute. The clouds moved, the light brightened, the mist went away, the falls ran out of water and became dribbles, the rainbow disappeared, and the humdrum of the canyon returned. It had been magic, and now the magic was gone.

Mogi and Frank hiked awhile more, zigzagging across the draw. But the rocks had become slick and the sand wet, so the plan of going around the whole mesa was abandoned, and they turned back.

"If we slow down, maybe we'll miss the kitchen chores for getting supper ready," Frank suggested. Mogi quickly agreed.

They crossed the draw and climbed the sloping ground at the bottom of the solitary mesa, looking for pools of water at the bottom of where the falls had been. Mogi led the way as they scrambled over the jumble of rocks and up through the still-soaked bushes, weeds, and grasses.

The heavy smell of the wet sagebrush was almost over-powering.

The bottom of the biggest waterfall, Mogi thought, should be a great place to find rocks for Mr. Jennings.

When he reached what he guessed was the right pool, he shoved his hand deep into the sand at the bottom and grabbed as many thumb-sized stones as he could. Frank held open a baggie as Mogi sifted out the sand and dumped his handful in.

Using his marker, Mogi wrote *waterfalls* across the top of the baggie and put a number *1* in the corner.

Then they moved to the next pool and put another handful in a different baggie. By the time they got back to camp, they were sure they would have enough rocks to send Mr. Jennings into a happy dance.

———

Above the two boys, high on a ledge of the stranded mesa, a pair of eyes watched them carefully. Peering through binoculars, the eyes grew narrow and focused as Mogi and Frank filled their bags from the pools and wandered back to camp.

The eyes watched Mogi lay the baggies on an empty river bag next to his tent. Then the two boys, salivating over the smell of grilling burgers, changed out of their wet clothes and quickly got in line for dinner.

In the distance, the eyes turned away and faded into the mesa.

CHAPTER 6

I t was an hour past midnight, and the harsh light of a full moon drained away the color and depth of the landscape, turning everything into a black-and-white still life.

But not all was still. Along the uneven floor of the draw, a lone figure slipped from rock to rock, slinked across the patches of open sand, and faded in and out of shadows.

Sweeping swiftly through the rough relief of the canyon, the figure drew close to the sleeping river camp.

Mogi was restless. The sand beneath him was hard and uneven, making his sleeping bag slip against the pad with any movement so that his body would jerk, then relax, then jerk again.

With sleep coming and going, he lay thinking about the pictures he had taken after the storm. He had pre-viewed them on the camera's tiny screen and had some clear favorites. Full-width on his monitor at home, they should be fabulous.

With visions of the pictures in his head, Mogi listened to Frank's breath, soft and rhythmic. The young Navajo had fallen asleep as soon as his head hit the pillow.

I wish I could sleep like that, Mogi thought.

Suddenly he was startled as a shadow passed over the wall of the tent.

A rustle of plastic, a shuffle, and it was gone.

Who was jacking with his stuff?

He hesitated and then fumbled with the zipper as he tried to open the tent without disturbing Frank. Sticking his head out, he glimpsed the shadow moving into the distance. It was headed up the draw, which meant that it wasn't any of the camp people.

Quickly pulling his running shoes on, not taking the time to tie the laces, he launched himself out the tent door. About fifty feet later, one shoe came off, but he kept going.

Mogi could barely see the figure in the distance. The boulders, bushes, and their shadows stood as light and dark objects, refusing to look different from the figure darting from one to the other.

Finally, he kicked his other shoe off and started a fast trot, watching carefully to keep to sand. Every now and then, he stepped on a rock and pulled up sharply as the pain stabbed him.

A few heartbeats later, the flitting shadow ahead of him was lost completely. The scene returned to a still life.

Mogi bent over to catch his breath. As his gasping slowed, he stood straight and realized he was cold. He hadn't given a thought to a shirt, a jacket, or even his pants.

Hoping no one was watching, he turned and started back, picking his way carefully.

The ghosts of the San Juan.

It popped into his mind like a forgotten memory.

————

"Do you see anything?"

"Nada. When he got close to any flat rocks, he must have stepped where he knew he wouldn't leave a footprint."

Mogi and Frank worked their way up the draw. Whoever it was had left clear footprints between the tent and the path out of the camp. A textured sole with large ridges around the outside and a broad heel. It was the print of a common work boot. Only about half the populace wore them around where Mogi lived.

The good news was that no one with the school trip had brought work boots, much less worn them. Mogi took a picture of the print in case he wanted to compare boot prints around the high school grounds.

"I don't understand it," Mogi said to Frank. "It doesn't make any sense. Why would someone steal our bags of rocks?"

"Maybe he was after the dry bag or something when you spooked him. It was probably a Navajo kid who smelled the burgers and couldn't resist coming down from the rim and checking us out."

"Do Navajo kids wear work boots?"

"Oh, well, I don't know many who do, cowboy boots mainly, but it wouldn't be that strange."

Mogi gave one last look at the solitary mesa. "I guess we'd better go back. It's probably time for breakfast."

Hating to leave, hating to have questions that weren't answered, Mogi turned and led the way back to camp.

For bags of rocks?

That's all he could figure was missing. He remembered tossing the baggies from the pools of water below the falls onto his dry bag outside the tent. After supper, he'd forgotten to put them with the other bags of rocks on the raft, but the morning light showed that they were nowhere to be found.

What would anyone want with bags of rocks?

It was as Mogi and Frank were folding their tent that he saw what the thief had missed. One of the baggies had slid off his dry bag and come to rest against the tent, covered by its edge as his sleeping bag shifted during the night. It was the baggie marked number 1, the rocks from the biggest waterfall.

He took a quick peek inside, saw nothing but pebbles, and sealed it back up. Then he tossed the baggie into the bottom of the tent bag and forgot about it.

———

"How would you like to try rowin' a boat?" Mr. Bottington asked. "Seems to me you've been mighty interested."

Mogi grew red in the face but accepted with a smile.

He had wanted to from the first day.

As the other rafts shoved off from shore, Mogi sat in the oarsman's seat of the equipment raft, barely able to see over the piles of equipment in front and in back of him. Mr. Bottington had rearranged the dry bags directly behind Mogi to make a seat for himself that offered almost armchair luxury.

"Okeedokee. The major thing is knowin' where the raft is in relation to the current. You can't go across the river if you're pointin' down- or upriver— you gotta be pointin' crossways. But you can't speed up or slow down if you're crossways, so you have to turn the boat if you want to do that."

As Mogi plunged the big oars into the river and pulled as hard as he could, the raft crept toward the center of the river.

He couldn't believe it was so difficult.

As he flailed at the water—the boat turning in circles, bumping the shore, bumping rocks, bumping sandbars, once getting stuck in the mud—Mogi felt foolish.

"You gotta be patient, son," Mr. Bottington said as he leaned back against the cushion of dry bags and put his hands behind his head. "It'll come. You'll learn to read the river, and it'll click. Give it time."

The river certainly looked different from his view as a passenger.

"Look over there," Mr. Bottington would point. "Look across the width of the river and see how the surface of the water changes. Think about how the water is followin' the land underneath."

Mogi gradually rowed more smoothly, understanding how to sometimes pull on the oars, sometimes not, sometimes pushing instead. He began to see the current, though it was hard when the river became wide and shallow.

The more he understood, the more he loved it.

Carefully, smoothly, deliberately, Mogi learned to make small adjustments instead of big ones, avoiding having to hurry and thrash the water to correct his direction at the last minute. He would row for an hour or so, then rest his muscles as Mr. Bottington took over, then take up the oars once more. They continued through the day like that, even when the river narrowed and became fast and rough in the rapids, with Mr. Bottington pointing out how the water showed the best way to go.

"I do believe you're a natural, son," Mr. Bottington said.

"Ya got a nice touch. You're beginnin' to see things before you get there. Maybe you'd like a job this summer."

CHAPTER 7

The camp that night was uneventful, but the next morning was not. Mr. Bottington gathered the oarsmen and drew an outline of Government Rapid in the sand, reminding them of the best way to enter it, where the major rocks lay, where to row hard, where to turn sideways and cross the waves, and how to miss the monstrous rock at the end of the run.

This was the worst rapid on the river, and they would be there in less than an hour.

Where the river ran through the middle section of the canyon, the rocky rim above had split and broken, sending several car-sized boulders crashing into the water. They not only rerouted the current for a hundred yards but also narrowed the river's channel to half its normal width.

Huge waves there tossed rafts up, down, and sideways if the pilots could not control their boats well enough.

As most of the students listened to Mr. Bottington's talk, a few circulated stories about previous school trips on which rafts were caught in the rocks, cut open by sharp edges, and turned sideways and flipped over in the big waves. Once, a raft had hit the big end rock head-on, pushing it straight into the air and tossing everyone into the churning waves. No one was seriously hurt, but the stories were enough to scare most of the listeners.

An hour later, Mogi, Jennifer, Becky, and Frank heard the rapid first, then spied the spray of water swirling above it. As the raft pulled closer, Mogi could swear that the rocks on each side of the water resembled the teeth of a mad dog. He slid off the tube with the others and knelt on the floor of the raft, their hands gripping the rope along the top of the tubes. The raft accelerated and then dropped into a crashing, swirling, kicking section of water with waves ten feet or more in height.

It was like being inside a washing machine.

The raft swooped up, crashed down, swung back and forth, slammed into the surface of the water, got pushed back into the air, and bucked under its passengers like a wild horse. Mogi and the others were hit by waves of water, drenching them, only to see more rocks and whitewater ahead.

Finally, staring upward as they shot past the tall rock at the end of the run, they were out of the rapid and cheering, turning in the raft to watch as others followed behind them. All were shouting the victory of having survived.

Running through another corner of the canyon immediately after the rapids, Mogi felt a significant drop in the speed of the water. As he looked ahead, the river turned slow and lazy, sometimes stretching from one side of the canyon to the other, winding its way past large stretches of sand bars. In places, the water was only inches deep, requiring some of the students to walk alongside the rafts. Then most of the students started walking through the water where they could.

They had reached the last stretch of the river. Mr. Jennings explained how Lake Powell had grown to its maximum size in 1984, backing up water into every one of its bordering canyons, including the San Juan's. The lake's calmer waters reached within two miles of Government Rapid. Without a strong current to carry the sediment-filled water away, the sediment settled out of the water, and the riverbed filled with dirt, clay, and sand.

In some places, the sediment reached thirty feet thick.

When the lake waters became lower in the following years, the river and its channel returned, now meandering slowly as it cut through the sediment that remained.

"Aaaii! Help!" suddenly came a cry from ahead.

Jennifer's friend Belinda had gotten out of her boat and been walking on the edge of a sand bar. Now she was stuck along its edge, her feet sinking into an area much darker than the sand.

Chuck, the oarsman of Mogi's raft, was laughing as he pulled closer.

"We call it Whale's Blubber," he said. "It's not so much quicksand as it is quickmud. Once you get in it, it's almost impossible to get out."

"Whale's Blubber?" Mogi asked. "Pretty dumb name."

Chuck laughed again. "Yeah, but it's easy to remember if you get caught in it. There's not much real quicksand on the river. Real quicksand happens when water has worn all the sharp edges off the grains of sand, so it's round and doesn't compact and slips all around your feet if you step in it. That's why you sink. Whale's Blubber is like that, but there's sediment mixed in, so it doesn't just slip around someone but sticks to their feet and legs like mud. It's almost impossible to fight the suction when you try to pull yourself out."

Though Belinda had sunk in only a foot or so, it was enough for the mud's grip to lock around her legs. Two boys from her raft had tried to rescue her but were sinking into the mud now themselves.

"Look all the way across this sandbar," Chuck said as he pointed. "It's all Blubber along the edge for seven or ten feet where the river keeps it wet. There're only one or two places on the river where the Blubber is like this. Everybody sit still, and we'll see if we can help."

He pulled back on his oars to slow down, then gradually maneuvered the raft up next to the struggling teens.

Mogi and Frank grabbed Belinda as she sat back onto the front tube while Jennifer and Becky poured water around her legs to thin the mud that had trapped her. It took most of twenty minutes, half-inch at a time, before she was able to use her weight and the aid of the other teens to pull her feet free from the suction, sacrificing her sandals to the depths of the mud. The two boys were not in so deep and came out more easily.

"If you have to cross Blubber," Chuck said, "the best thing is to lie down and roll across it, so no particular body part pokes under the surface and gets pulled in."

The couple of hours left of the trip were uneventful, made better by the warm sun and lack of rain. The high, stepped, broken-rock walls of the canyon gradually sank under the level of the river, bringing the top layer of thick rock down to its surface. The river became a narrow channel curving between skyscraper-tall walls of sheer rock rising straight out of the water.

No longer having a shore to land on, the rafts stayed with the current of the river. The students took photographs from the boats and recorded the GPS information, but the rock sampling was abandoned. It was now one long, continuous layer of the same kind of rock.

Rounding the last corner of the canyon on the last day, Mogi, Jennifer, Becky, and Frank could see the river straighten into a wide, flat countryside. The deep canyon walls completed their descent into the land's surface and disappeared. Looking back toward where they had come, it seemed impossible that they'd rafted past two-thousand-foot canyon walls.

An hour later, the rafts landed on a stretch of empty bank, a parking lot not more than a hundred yards away.

Taking buckets of water from the river, the students washed the caked mud off the rafts as well as they could.

A bus with a flat trailer soon arrived, and they all worked together, stacking the still-inflated rafts on the trailer and tying them down while the equipment, bags, and boxes were hoisted into huge metal racks on top of the bus.

As they started the long trip back on a tortuously washed-out dirt road, it wasn't long before most everyone had fallen asleep.

CHAPTER 8

The first week back at school, Mr. Jennings downloaded the digital pictures from the school cameras onto his computer. Using a special program, he sorted the pictures and then merged them to make several panoramas of the river walls. Overlapping the panoramas, he pasted prints on a gym wall close to the entrance. Maybe seventy feet long, the result was a surprisingly real view of the entire San Juan canyon. The rock layers, rising or falling from the beginning of the trip to the end, were clearly seen and easy to follow.

The best photographs, however, were the ones taken by Mogi right after the thunderstorm. Mr. Jennings was so impressed that he made large color prints and mounted them together inside the glass of the trophy case in the gym's foyer. Together, the pictures made a panorama almost three feet long that showcased the waterfalls, the camp, and the rainbow above the river. The features were amazingly clear, and the colors were extraordinary.

Mogi couldn't help but walk by them every day.

The geology class sorted the hundreds of bags of rocks, picking out a few samples that were typical of the locations where they had been found and ordering them according to the GPS locations. The rocks were then taped below the giant display of the canyon on the gym wall.

Everyone in school was impressed by how well Mr. Jennings's exercise had worked out.

That Friday in geology class, he held up a small plastic bag and told the students, "Somebody came back with a really unusual bag of rocks from the vent pipe and needs to get extra credit. Does anybody recognize this bag of rocks?"

It had *waterfall* written across the top, with the number *1* marked clearly beside it, and Mogi and Frank said it was the first one they had filled at the stranded mesa.

Burl Bottington had brought it by after finding it in the bottom of a tent bag while cleaning the equipment.

After pouring the rocks onto his work bench, it took him only a few seconds to realize what some of them were.

Grinning a devilish grin, he sacked them up and made the drive to Mr. Jennings's house.

As the students watched, Mr. Jennings spread a paper towel on a lab table and emptied the bag. He had washed out the sand, mud, and gravel. Most of what was left were large pebble-sized rocks that looked no different than the others.

But four of the rocks did look different: Two were nickel-sized and bloodred in color, the third was a thumb-sized chunk of green glass, and the fourth looked blue, coated with rounded bumps of chalky white.

"These two," Mr. Jennings said as he passed them around, "are red garnets, semi-precious stones that are the largest I've seen. But this," he held up the green rock, "is the biggest find of the year. This is called green glass. You guys did a great job at the vent pipe."

"Uh, none of these came from the vent pipe," Mogi said. "We found them at the bottom of the waterfalls where we camped. Next to the stranded mesa."

Mr. Jennings gave the look that teachers typically give when no one has the obvious answer to their question.

"No, they'd have to come from the vent pipe. That's the only place you'd find them along the San Juan. Maybe you switched baggies or something."

He returned to talking to the whole class.

"Now, if the green one is the biggest find of the year, this blue one is the strangest one of the year." He held up the fourth rock. "I'm pretty sure I know what it is, but to find a rock like this is so far out of normal that maybe I'm wrong about what it is. Fortunately, we have an expert with us."

He handed it to Becky. "What do you think it is?"

"It's turquoise!" she said with surprise, handing it to Frank, who agreed.

"That's what I thought, too," Mr. Jennings said, "which makes it the most surprising of the four. Where it came from, I don't have a clue. Turquoise has never been found along the San Juan. I suppose that it might have been part of the vent hole, but it's more likely it was dropped by some wandering native. I'm going to put it, the red garnets, and the green glass in the display cabinet to keep it safe.

"Did you all know that turquoise was once more valuable than gold? In fact, did you know that around 1900, turquoise was worth more than a hundred times the same amount of gold? And did you know..."

Mogi was trying to get his attention, but it wasn't working.

"...some of the largest turquoise mines are in Iran and China? And the Egyptians had turquoise mines in the Sinai Peninsula?"

Mr. Jennings could go on for the whole period like this, so Mogi decided to jump in.

"Mr. Jennings," he said quickly and loudly, "I brought back a couple of big rocks from the vent pipe, but I didn't pick up anything from there that was this small. I can show you exactly where I got these—it's in one of the pictures taped up in the trophy case."

"Let me see," Mr. Jennings said, opening the class-room door, then following Mogi down the hall. The rest of the class drifted behind them to the display of photographs taped together in the glass case. Mogi had no problem identifying the biggest waterfall. He pointed to the pool at its bottom.

"Frank held the baggie open while I scooped rocks

out of the pool of water at the bottom. We also got handfuls out of these," he said as he moved his finger to the other waterfalls. "But I marked the baggies with different numbers."

Mr. Jennings was obviously not convinced, but Mogi and Frank both agreed on the location.

"Well," Mr. Jennings said, "I guess I'll have to think about this. Something isn't making sense."

The students moved toward the classroom. But when Mogi looked back, he saw Frank continuing to stare at the photograph. It was a minute later that he came back to the classroom.

He was pale and didn't notice when others turned to talk to him. When the bell sounded, he quickly moved out the door and down the hall.

Frank was gone from the next class and didn't show up after school.

Something was wrong.

———

Jennifer huffed into Mogi's room after she came home from school with Frank and Becky.

"That was a lowdown dirty trick!"

He looked up in confusion.

"I don't know why you did it, dork-boy, but that was just mean! You know Frank and Becky are pretty sensitive about this ghost business, and then you had to go off and sneak in something like this. It was a rotten thing to do, and you need to apologize to them."

The last words were said with her face two inches from his.

"What are you talking about? I haven't done anything!" was all he could manage.

"You know what I'm talking about, and it is *not* funny," Jennifer said as she stormed out of his room.

"What? What? You've got to tell me what I've done or it's not fair," he said as he followed her into her room.

"The guy in the picture, that's what, you snake!"

"What guy? What picture?" Mogi said as she turned around and passed him in the doorway. She went back into his room, sat at his computer, which was always on, brought up his pictures of the waterfalls and rainbow, clicked on one in particular, and brought it up on the screen.

"This guy!" she said as she pointed.

Mogi walked over and looked at the picture. Scooting her out of his chair, he went to another screen, brought up an image processing application, copied in the picture, and enlarged it.

He didn't understand, but there was no denying it.

A man was standing at the top of the big waterfall, looking directly at Mogi as the picture was taken.

Mogi leaned back in his chair and put his hands behind his head, his feelings numb as he tried to remember anything at all from the moment he'd taken the picture.

Jennifer glanced at him, then looked at the image on the screen and knew that nothing had been done to the picture.

What she saw was what was there.

"Oooooohhhhh dear," she said as she slowly sat down on the edge of Mogi's bed, feeling numb like her brother. Her heartbeat was strong enough that she heard it in her ears.

The man in the picture.

A ghost of the San Juan.

CHAPTER 9

Dressed in a blue parka with the hood over his head and hands in his pockets, the man appeared as a hazy painting. The mist in the air had scattered the light, so the image was not sharp and the colors not bright.

"Let's see if we can clean him up a little," Mogi said as he clicked on his computer's tool icons. Heightening the contrast, enhancing the brightness, using a filter for focusing—each time, the image became a little clearer. It may have been an effect of the software, but the man's face began to have sharp features, and, in particular, the eyes became startlingly intense.

Mogi pressed a button and his color printer whirred into action.

———

"It doesn't look like a ghost, unless they've traded in their white sheets for parkas," Jennifer said as she held the printout in her hands. "We can probably throw out that idea. As for how he got there, I don't suppose he could have climbed?"

"He'd have to fly," Frank said. "The ledges don't look tall from across the draw, but they must be ten or twenty feet straight up."

"You think he was the guy who stole your rocks?" Becky asked.

"I don't know," Mogi said. "He could have gotten off the ledge if he had a rope, but getting up would take long enough. He couldn't have done it without me seeing him in the moonlight. I guess he could have hid in the bushes and climbed up later, but why would he bother? What would he do when he got there? Maybe he just kept going down the draw."

"Maybe we should think about why he was there instead of how he got there," Jennifer said. "It seems to me that if he's up there, he's up there for a reason."

"And that would be?" Mogi asked.

"Well, he's a tourist out for a climb. Or he's an anthropologist looking for ruins. Or he's a geologist looking at rocks. Or he's a Navajo looking for lost livestock."

"Oh, good. That's really productive. Maybe he's Superman and he's resting on his way to Metropolis."

"Well, excuuuuuse me," Jennifer shot back.

"I'm glad it's Friday," Becky said, standing up between the siblings. "Because that means I get to go see my grandmother tomorrow. My dad's working and my mom's coming tonight to get me, but Frank's staying here, so maybe he can help Mogi get this worked out by Monday, okay?"

"Can I go with you?" Jennifer asked. Then she quickly added, "Just kidding, but once my brother starts in on something he doesn't understand, he'll drive everybody nuts until he solves it."

"Oh, yeah?" Mogi said. "Well, it just so happens that I'm going mountain biking in the canyons on Sunday afternoon to think great thoughts, commune with nature, understand the great cosmic forces of the universe, and I'm taking Frank with me. Between the two of us, we'll figure out this guy in no time."

Frank looked dazed.

"You weren't doing anything special Sunday afternoon, were you?" Mogi asked Frank.

"I didn't think so, but I'm trying to think of something as fast as I can."

"Good. That settles it. You can use my bike and I'll take my dad's. We'll be off on another adventure."

———

"You're kidding."

"No, really," Mogi said. "You put one foot into this hole and your other foot in this one. See how the holes alternate up to the platform? That's how the Anasazi climbed. Right up the side of the rock onto that platform. Then they followed the ledge to where the ruins are. It's a lot easier than it looks."

"That's thirty feet straight up. You've got to be kidding," Frank said again.

"Here, watch me do it."

Riding mountain bikes back into the canyons north of Bluff, it had taken about thirty minutes to reach Mogi's canyon. He thought of it as his canyon anyway. He had found it last summer.

"See, one foot after the other." Mogi stepped onto a platform high above Frank's head. "And I'm here. Go ahead, try it."

Frank was sure-footed and had the natural ability of someone who lives close to the land. A minute later, Mogi moved aside to let Frank onto the wooden platform tucked into a wide crack in the rock face.

"I had to make the footholds a little deeper because of the erosion. And it took me a whole week of hauling scrap wood from my house to make this platform."

It was a safe place to stop and look back at the rocks and crevices of the canyon and out over the flat land beyond. From there, the two boys followed a wide rock shelf around a corner into a deep-set rock alcove. Up against the back of the alcove was an ancient Anasazi ruin.

"How'd you find this place?" Frank asked.

"I bike a lot in the canyons. Kind of my hobby, I guess.

"I love to explore. Anyway, I go up any canyon I find. I found this one, checked it out to the end, then saw this on the way back. Took me quite a while to figure out how they got up here. That was my challenge—seeing if I could figure it out and then doing it myself."

They walked close to the ruin, looking at the sandstone floor and ceiling. The rock ceiling made a long, graceful, upward arc from the back of the alcove, curved out over the canyon, and then shot straight up in a hundred-foot wall. The alcove floor was fifty feet wide and maybe twenty feet deep. Everything was colored tan and light brown.

The ruin held seven rooms with walls made of stacked sandstone blocks. Built from floor to ceiling, each room stood about eight feet high in the front and shrank to nothing as the walls tucked into the alcove's floor along the back.

Frank squatted as he looked through the short doorways. There were three side rooms, entered by a doorway from a main room and probably used for storage or sleeping. He could see small piles of corncobs in the corners.

Everything was loose dirt, mud, or stone and gave off a dry, dusty aroma.

"I haven't messed with anything," Mogi said. "I can't believe that I'm the first to ever find this, so I'm guessing that it's all been picked over. I also didn't dig anywhere."

"That's good," Frank said. "You don't want to dig. Lots of bodies were buried in the floors of ruins, and you don't want to mess with the dead or wherever they lived."

Mogi looked at him with a sudden concern. "Oh, great. I'm sorry. Do we need to get out of here?"

"Nah. My grandfather would have never come into the canyon if he'd known there were ruins. My dad might climb up, but he wouldn't go into the rooms. I guess I'm the next generation and I don't have feelings one way or the other. I doubt that after a few hundred years there're any *chindi*, any spirits of the dead, left. On the other hand, let's not dig up any bones."

"I don't have any bones," Mogi replied, "and wouldn't want to look for any. But there's a special place I want to show you. I've never heard of another one like it."

Mogi walked to the end of the alcove, where there was a vertical crack in the rock face. Close to the floor was a triangular opening pointing upward, about three feet tall.

Mogi knelt, took off his daypack, threw it into the opening, and crawled through. Nervously, Frank crawled in after him.

The opening was only a couple of feet long, and the two boys soon found themselves in a small circular room.

But instead of a ceiling, Frank could see a patch of sky above. The whole room was the bottom of a circular shaft scooped out of the sandstone cliff. He backed up to a wall and sat next to Mogi. There were no pieces of pottery, no rocks or bricks, no writing on the walls. It was empty and barren. Besides being covered with windswept leaves, pine needles, sand, dirt, and dust, the floor was as smooth as a mud pie left to dry.

Frank was silent, looking around. He closed his eyes.

Scooting out and sitting up straight, he stretched his arms out from his side and held his palms open. Mogi watched as he took deep breaths.

When Frank opened his eyes, Mogi finally spoke: "What did you just do?"

"Oh," Frank said, a little embarrassed. "I grew up watching my grandfather get up every morning, go outside, and face the rising sun. He'd put his arms out like that. He'd tell me about welcoming the day, about putting his arms out to receive whatever the sun was bringing to him. He'd do it at night too, especially when the moon was coming up. I kind of do it when I find something special. Try to accept what's happening and let it in."

"You did that on the river, in the draw after the rain shower. You closed your eyes and put your arms out."

"I did? I remember it being pretty special, so I probably did."

"Do you feel anything? I mean, does something happen? You glow or shake or vibrate?"

Frank laughed. "I'm pretty sure I don't glow. I don't think anything happens, but I'm not really expecting anything.

"Well," Frank added slowly, "maybe I am. We have a word—*hozho*—a word that doesn't go into English very well, but *harmony* comes pretty close. It means that everything is in order, everything's where it should be, where it ought to be. If you don't have *hozho*, then you have disorder—everything's out of place, not natural. Uncomfortable. Things aren't right.

"Letting special things in reminds me to be balanced, to have *hozho*. I want to be open, ready to receive what the spirits are bringing."

"Wow. Maybe I ought to try it sometime."

"Couldn't hurt. 'Course, maybe you white guys glow when you do it," Frank said with a small smile.

———

It was late afternoon when Frank said goodbye at Mogi's house. Watching him walk away, Mogi considered the afternoon a success even without solving the mystery of The Man in the Blue Parka. But it was too early to quit for the day. After riding in the sandy canyon bottoms, the smoothness of the pavement had felt good, and he decided to keep going for a while. He rolled his bike out of the garage and was at full speed by the end of the block.

From the seat of a bicycle, there wasn't a whole lot to Bluff, but Mogi made the best of what there was. Going up side streets, across parking lots, down Main Street, back out on the access road, over around the water tower.

Feeling free, he thought. Can't beat it. Wonder if you can find *hozho* on a mountain bike? Maybe feeling free is *hozho*.

He turned at an intersection to take the long way home. The route would go behind the high school, across the basketball courts, down the path next to the drainage channel, and back around to his house.

Glancing as he circled past the rear of the gym, he

saw that one of the back doors was partly open. It brought back memories. Part of basketball was the constant reminders by the coach to make sure all the doors were shut after practice was over.

Hopping off his bike, Mogi trotted over to close the metal door.

But the door had not been left open, it had been broken open. Looking closely, not touching anything, he saw big gouges where the door had been pried from its frame.

Silent now, listening, holding his breath, he heard noises coming from inside. Glass was breaking. The tinkling, crashing sounds were unmistakable.

Mogi took a deep breath, carefully opened the door enough for his lanky body to squeeze through, and slipped past the doorway into the gym. Instead of the sharp, explosive sound of glass falling to the floor, now he heard the grinding of its being stepped on.

The sound was coming from the other side of the swinging doors that separated the gym from the front entry hall. Thinking of what was in the hall, Mogi realized that the only glass was in the trophy case along the side wall.

Why in the world would someone break that? It's not like the trophies were worth anything.

He moved next to the bleachers and crept forward.

Carefully. Quietly.

The crunching noise stopped.

Mogi's heart was pumping up into his throat. Trying to keep his breath from being too loud, he slipped up to the swinging doors of the front hall, pushing one of them slowly, straining to see through the crack. Slowly, he pushed it more, just a little more.

Whang! The door slammed into him, knocking him sprawling to the floor. As his head hit the gym floor, a dark figure darted through the doorway and stopped to look at him, then took the large crowbar he was carrying and jabbed it hard into Mogi's chest as he lay there. A sharp stab of pain arched across his body, and he rolled away from the figure, holding his hand over his chest. He felt blood seeping into his shirt as the hurt grew into an angry burn.

Rolling back, he saw a man in a black, hooded sweat-shirt sprinting across the room and out the back door.

Mogi struggled to get up, once, twice. Finally standing, hunkered over, holding his chest, tears streaming down his face, he ran with a half-shuffle toward the doors. When he stumbled through, there was no one in sight. Whoever it was had disappeared. From the other side of the school, he heard a squealing of tires, the shifting of gears, and then silence.

Man, it hurt! Mogi painfully lowered himself onto the sidewalk and pressed his hand against the wound. He felt the tear in his T-shirt and the flap of skin where the sharp edge of the crowbar had gouged through it to the bone.

He rolled over on his back, a little bewildered about what to do. It was going to hurt to ride home. He'd tell his folks what happened, they'd call the police and the school, and then he'd come back to the school to repeat everything he'd heard and seen.

Might as well get it over with.

Mogi lifted himself up, wincing as he felt his shirt-front sopped with blood, and shuffled toward his bike, hunched over in pain. As his eyes glanced across the ground, he stopped suddenly and backed up.

In the loose dirt next to the sidewalk, a footprint had been left by the fleeing man—a footprint Mogi had seen before. A textured sole with large ridges around the outside and a broad heel.

The ghost was back.

CHAPTER 10

The news was all over school by the time Mogi got to class in the morning. The evening before was what he had expected, but he had also gotten a trip to the emergency room, where a doctor put seven stitches in his chest.

Now he not only hurt but also smelled like a medicine cabinet because of the bandages and antiseptic.

Yellow police tape had been used to mark the gym and its foyer off-limits, as well as the back doors and a large part of the back of the school. Mogi had been interviewed as soon as he was patched up, and went back to the school with two officers to point out the details of what happened. The principal and Mr. Jennings were there. Not only had the trophy case been broken into, but the geology lab and storeroom also had been ransacked.

Rocks were dumped out of drawers, filing cabinets opened, papers strewn about, and specimen cabinets broken into. The boxes of samples had been toppled and opened, and the hundreds of bags were scattered around the floor.

"It's going to take weeks to get everything back where it belongs," Mr. Jennings said as they picked their way across the floor. "I have to do that before I can figure out what the thief took."

"Uh, I have a guess, if you want to check something," Mogi said.

"What's that?"

"Where did you put the rocks that were in my baggie? The ones from the waterfall?"

Mr. Jennings moved rocks out of the way with his shoe as he turned to the display cabinet on the wall. The glass had been smashed, and the waterfall rocks were gone.

"How'd you know that?" Mr. Jennings asked.

"Just a lucky guess," was all Mogi could say. He'd known the rocks would be gone, even if he didn't understand why. He was even sure that all the other damage in the room was done only as a coverup. Whoever made the footprint outside had come back to get the rocks from the pool. Mr. Jennings had bragged about the red, green, and blue rocks for a week, even posting a picture on Facebook. It didn't go viral or anything like that, but anyone could have known about them.

There's something about those rocks, Mogi thought.

But what? They were valuable gems but not that valuable.

It had to be something about where they were

found—maybe. Was something else in that pool of water at the foot of the mesa? Was somebody afraid that we'd go back and look?

————

"You're looking depressed, dork-boy," Jennifer said.

Mogi sat at his desk at home. His sister had come into the room and sat on the bed with a pillow behind her scrunched up against the wall.

"Yeah."

"How's your chest?"

"It hurts. I don't know if it's the stitches or the hair that the bandage is pulling out."

"Yet another advantage to being a girl—no chest hairs!"

Mogi moved his chair away from the desk and leaned forward, his head cupped in his hands.

"So, tell me something, my irrepressible sister. You believe in ghosts?"

"Are you cereal?"

"Yeah."

"Not at all. Is that what's bothering you?"

"Look at these." Mogi took two pictures and laid them on the corner of his desk. Each showed the outline of a boot print.

"This one is from the river trip. This one I took yesterday at the gym. Same boot print, same boot. Things are adding up here, and I'm really confused. First, there's an ancient mystery of four guys who vanish on a rafting trip but leave their ghosts haunting the river canyon. Then there's a thief on the river who takes bags of rocks and leaves a boot print.

"Then the bag he *doesn't* take turns up with semi-precious stones that Mr. Jennings is convinced shouldn't have been found where they were found. Then there's some guy in a blue parka standing in a place that only a bird or a ghost could get to, directly above where I found the stones.

"Now there's yesterday. A guy wearing the same boots steals those same stones. I don't get it. I can't help but feel all this starts with that expedition in 1934. What could possibly be happening today that's related to those four guys?"

"It can't be related," Jennifer said. "You've got two events that only look like they're related. It's a coincidence. Forget the mystery of the four guys. There are no ghosts. Now you've only got a man who flies and is obsessed with red, green, and blue rocks.

"See—much simpler!"

———

No. Not simpler at all.

Jennifer went to bed but Mogi wasn't even close to sleepy. He took her place on his bed, scrunched up his pillow even more, and leaned his head against the wall.

What he hadn't told Jennifer was that he was scared. Why he thought there was danger, he wasn't quite sure, but the pain in his chest didn't come from an accident. That crowbar, he felt sure, wasn't meant to wound. It was meant to kill.

He printed another picture of Mr. Parka. Looking at the man's eyes gave him chills.

Okay, he thought, I may be scared, but I don't think you're a ghost, and I don't believe in coincidences. You're connected to whatever happened in 1934, to that stranded mesa, and to those rocks.

I just don't understand how.

Mogi moved to the table beside his desk and cleared it off. He pulled a tablet of paper out of the desk drawer and focused his thoughts. What do I know?

He wrote it all down.

1. The bashed-up boat hanging from the ceiling.

2. The story about the four men in 1934—a geologist named Gordon Kattrick and three locals.

3. The disappearance of the men: no camps, no bodies.

4. The report from the oil company about the unusual rocks from the 1933 canyon survey.

5. Those rocks were found at the vent pipe.

7. The baggie of precious stones.

Mogi added to the list, remembering each occurrence or piece of information in the last month that might be relevant. His mother had always told him his memory was a gift, and it was, he supposed. It seemed that he remembered everything he saw, did, or heard, which let him play back things in his mind like a movie. It was great for taking tests because he could remember pages from textbooks and things his teachers had said.

The bad part was that his brain was stuffed with information that refused to be forgotten. Good things, bad things, not-good-not-bad things. Information and images he took in didn't automatically separate themselves into bins of meaningful and not meaningful, so Mogi had to do the sorting himself.

Sometimes, he felt he was drowning in information.

But today, right now, it was valuable and important. From cleaning Mr. Bottington's hangar a few weeks ago to looking at the man in the picture a few minutes ago—what had happened? What did he know? What did he not know?

Mogi kept writing.

8. Was there anything special about the two boats? Who's Norm Nevills?

9. Who were the other three men? They were local men —didn't anybody notice they were missing? How long did it take?

10. Can I find newspaper articles about the other three men? Police reports?

11. If the precious stones from the stranded mesa can only come from a vent pipe, could they have come from the vent pipe that Mr. Jennings took us to? How would they have gotten from there to the mesa?

12. Is there another vent pipe on the San Juan? Has anyone found diamonds in any vent pipe in the Southwest?

The list grew to multiple pages, but it helped Mogi to see everything that he knew and didn't know. He put pictures of the stranded mesa next to the enlargement of Mr. Parka and the pictures of the boot print.

13. How did the man get to the ledge?

14. How did he get down, if he was the thief in the night?

15. How would he have gotten back up to the ledge?

16. What's so important about the rocks?

17. What's the fear of the rocks being found that he would want them back so badly?

18. How would a piece of turquoise ever be around that mesa?

Mogi stood up and looked at his piles of notes.

An hour later, he shoved them together, dumped them on the desk, and crawled between the sheets of his bed, defeated.

———

I can't do this, Mogi thought as he slumped in his seat.

I'm going to keel over right here in class. I can't make it.

He ached badly. His chest was throbbing, and he was tired. Really tired. His eyes were killing him. He had spent hours with his lists and then didn't sleep at all. He was managing to keep his eyes open in class, but controlling his mind was out of the question.

Mogi jerked himself up into a sitting position, but gradually, his head sank back down until it hit the desk.

It was raining hard before the waterfalls came, and suddenly they were there, oceans of water flowing down the side of the mesa, the man in the parka standing still as the water rushed by him.

Frank had his arms out to his sides while the camera was clicking away, the water rushing down into the catch basin where Mogi had his hand, scooping out rocks and putting them into a baggie, which Mr. Jennings was holding up and saying how great it was that somebody had found gems in the vent pipe, but Mogi knew they weren't from there. The man in the parka had given him the gems, throwing them over the ledge until they crashed into the glass of the trophy case, spilling all the trophies on the floor.

The ringing of the school bell woke him, but people were staring at him. They were looking down at him because he was looking up at them.

Why was he on the floor?

CHAPTER 11

"Glad to have you back, little brother," Jennifer said.

Mogi looked up at her from his bed and tried to act silly, but it hurt to laugh. "Glad to be back," he finally said.

The doctor had said his passing out was probably a delayed reaction to the stress added to the strong antibiotic he'd been given. He was sent home to sleep.

Jennifer gave him a hug. "Don't do that again. I'm going to my room to read, but I'm here. Call me if you need something."

Mogi carefully stretched his back and neck, took several deep breaths, which hurt, slid to the side of the bed, and slowly stood up. The piles of papers and photographs were still on the desk, but he passed them with only a glance as he walked to the bathroom and then to the refrigerator.

It took a few minutes of wolfing down a serious sandwich and a bottle of Dr Pepper before he felt better. The meal made quite a difference. Mogi could stand upright and walk back to his room without feeling a hundred years old.

Next to his desk, he took a deep breath.

Hozho.

Order and balance. Things where they should be.

He closed his eyes. He felt achy and tired, but not like before. The pressure was gone. Even the fear was gone. It will all work out, he thought. It's just a mystery with a lot of different views. It will all work out.

Relax, Mogi told himself. Think about good things. I don't have to save the world today. I've been out of balance, and I need to get into balance.

Breathe in, breathe out.

I'm happy Frank is my friend. And Becky. And I'm happy Jennifer is my sister, and that this is my home. I have been blessed.

He kept his eyes closed and thought more. Breathe in, breathe out. Balance. Order. Get my stuff together.

He thought of Frank.

Closing his door, Mogi stood in the middle of his room, straightened his shoulders, closed his eyes, and held his arms out from his sides, palms open. It hurt like crazy, but he did it gradually enough that the pain was tolerable.

Appreciate specialness. Ready to let in the specialness that's before me, around me, in me. Open and receiving.

I'm glad to be alive. I really am. The canyons are

special, the ruins are cool, this whole country is some-thing else, and I get to be here.

He took several deep breaths, rolled his head around, stretched his neck.

Relax. Let the specialness become part of me, make me special in return.

My rocks were like the samples from the oil company.

Mogi's eyes opened. What? Where did that thought come from?

The rock samples of the oil company. What had Mr. Jennings said?

Mogi went to his desk and sorted through the pages he had written, looking for the references to the rocks.

The ones gathered on the oil exploration showed that the samples from Mr. Jennings's vent pipe were extraordinary compared with previous years. More semi-precious stones than usual. Green and red stones. Really unusual.

Just like my bag of rocks. The rocks that Mr. Jennings said could come only from a vent pipe, so they had to come from the vent pipe we were at.

But they didn't. They came from the waterfall.

The oil company's rock samples might have come from there too.

Suddenly, a story was growing in Mogi's mind.

He sat at his computer and pulled up the enlarge-ment of Mr. Parka, clicked on the magnifying glass icon, and moved it around the figure. Going past the man's legs, he saw something he hadn't noticed before. Thank goodness for the camera's high resolution.

When Mogi clicked and enlarged the image even more, he realized what he was looking at.

Aha! That's how you got up there, Mr. Parka.

And I bet I know why too.

———

"He came from inside the mesa."

Mogi's three companions looked across his bedroom at him with bewildered faces. It was the next day, after school.

"Look at the side of the mesa after the rainstorm,"

Mogi said as he put copies of the waterfall pictures together in front of them. "See how much water there is in the big waterfall? Now look at the other waterfalls.

"They're much smaller. The rain falls on each ledge and overflows to the next ledge. Add that amount to the rain falling on that ledge itself, and you ought to see little waterfalls at the top, medium waterfalls in the middle, and large waterfalls at the bottom.

"These waterfalls are that way," he said as he pointed to several in the pictures. "The water coming from above joins the water below, making larger waterfalls as they cascade from one ledge to the next. Now look back at the biggest one."

The difference was obvious. On the cliff face above the figure of the man were one or two small waterfalls along the ledges, but the waterfall at his feet was a wide stream of water gushing over the edge, much bigger than rain falling on the ledge would have produced.

"That water is coming from someplace other than the rocks above. There had to be some source of water on the ledge itself, and that brings us to *this* picture."

Mogi held a printout of the enlargement he had made the day before. It was obviously the parka guy, but his legs were highlighted.

"Look at the wall behind his knees." Mogi touched his finger to the paper.

His audience crowded in. Behind and below the man, on his left, peeking above the waterfall, was a thick, curved slice of black. From Mogi's camera position on the opposite side of the draw, he had caught the upper part of a dark spot behind the man. Had Mogi been in the bottom of the draw, rather than up the opposite slope a little, the slice of black would not have appeared.

"That, my friends, is some kind of opening in the rock face. It has to be the source of the water. If this is a cave, and the water is coming from the cave, then the cave must lead to someplace where the rain funnels into it.

"I'm betting that the cave leads up to the next ledge or even two. That would make the rain funnel through the mesa rather than spill from one ledge to the next.

"It could, I suppose, even be a cave that goes all the

way to the top of the mesa, maybe like a split in the rock.

"And wherever the water is coming from is where the man came from. That's how he got to the ledge without ladders or ropes. There must be some kind of tunnel system inside the mesa.

"And there's some other things you ought to know too," Mogi said as he leaned forward and put his elbows on his knees.

"Remember the vent pipe that we worked on during the raft trip? Where the gasses and lava spurted through the surface of the earth, then fell back on itself and left the mountain of black rock? Well, there's another one. It's someplace inside that mesa Mr. Parka is standing on.

"That's why the four men made that trip in 1934. They went down the river to search for diamonds."

Jennifer smiled.

"Uh," she said, "you need more sleep."

"And not only that, but the geologist murdered the other guys to keep it a secret."

"I like that even better!" Jennifer said as she laughed.

Frank and Becky didn't laugh.

"You think this opening leads into the mesa, and from inside the mesa is where the rocks came from?" Frank asked, pointing to the slice of black above the waterfall.

Mogi nodded. "I figure that the opening leads to a big cave where there's a second vent pipe. Over the years, the water washed the colored stones out of the lava, out the opening, into the waterfall, and then into the pool of water at the bottom. That's how they ended up in our plastic bags."

"And the geologist guy found it when he was working for the oil company?" Becky asked. "You think this is where the turquoise came from?"

"Yeah. I figure the guy was doing his usual geology thing. He probably found stones like I did, started looking around, and discovered the opening. Then he went inside, found the vent pipe, and realized what he'd found but decided not to tell the others he was with. Instead, he took samples from the vent pipe and marked them as being found at Mr. Jennings's vent pipe that we went to so he could have the samples analyzed. That's why the rock report by the oil company was so different from the times before.

"The next year, in 1934, he goes back. He hires some local guys to take him down the river and back to the mesa. Remember that Mr. Jennings told us about the vent pipes in Africa being where the big diamond mines are?

"It was the same here. The guy was hoping that the vent pipe would have diamonds.

"When he makes it back to the vent pipe, the geologist kills the others so they can't tell. He hides the bodies inside, erases all their tracks, and then takes the two boats down the river. He bashes one in so it looks like they all died in a river accident and then uses the other one to escape."

"I think you've escaped, too," Jennifer said as she stood up. "You got your brain scrambled when you hit your head on the gym floor. You think all of this is true? A vent pipe would have exploded that mesa to bits! Remember?

"Volcano? Volcanoes go boom!"

"Well, maybe it was just a small one," Mogi said. "Or maybe the top of the mesa is where it came out. Remember that Mr. Jennings said a stranded mesa may never have had any humans on top of it? Maybe it's always been there and nobody's ever discovered it."

"Well, I think this is dumb. There's not a way in the world you can figure out the truth," she said flatly.

"Yes, there is," Mogi answered.

He watched their eyes and gave them a second to focus on him.

"We can go back to the mesa. We can go inside that opening and see what's there."

CHAPTER 12

Jennifer was absolutely, positively, without question, not going. No way. It wasn't until Becky begged her that she began to waffle.

Becky's insistence surprised both Mogi and Jennifer.

They were used to being at cross-purposes with each other: Mogi was adventurous and passionate about solving problems, while Jennifer was cautious and stuck closer to reality. Having a third person who was more passionate than either of them was something new.

"I know why," Jennifer said that night. "It's the turquoise.

"She'll go to the ends of the earth if she thought there was a new vein of turquoise inside that mesa. It could be the key to getting her dad back to the work that he loves and could even be a source of helping all the Navajo artisans."

"All based on that little rock?" he asked.

"You mean this little rock?" she said as she reached into her pocket and produced a gleaming stone.

Mogi looked closely. It was beautiful: a deep, rich, lustrous blue with tiny threads of gold.

"Mr. Jennings let Becky take it to her dad. It wasn't in the display case when it was broken into, so the thief never got it. Becky's dad put it on his polishing machine, took off the chalk, ground out the bumps, and then polished it. He said it was the finest stone he'd ever seen and that it was unique. He'd never seen any like it."

"Wow."

"Yeah. And if Becky thinks there's a source of turquoise in that mesa, she'd dig a hole all by herself to get to it. If we don't go with her, she and Frank will go by themselves."

"Uh, oh," Mogi said. "That sounds like we have to really do this."

"Uh, yeah, you dork. It was fun to imagine going back to the mesa, but now you need to figure out how to do it for real. Looks like you've gotten us into another adventure. I just hope you know what you're doing."

Taking a deep breath, Mogi threw himself into making what preparations he could, the rest of it was up to Burl Bottington and San Juan River Expeditions.

The four conspirators needed a raft.

They'd have to work fast. Luckily, the coming weekend was a long one, with teachers having an in-service training day on Monday. If they left after school on Friday, rowing instead of drifting, they could make the long trip with two camps, have time for exploring the mesa, and still have Monday to clean up the equipment before they had to be back to school on Tuesday.

It wasn't summer yet, so Mr. Bottington's business had few customers. He should have plenty of rafts available.

All he had to do was agree to lend them one.

———

"It was just a great trip! We want to do it again!" Mogi said as enthusiastically as he could to the big man sitting at his table in the storage building. Jennifer, Frank, and Becky nodded their agreement.

Mr. Bottington usually welcomed young people wanting to raft down the San Juan, but Mogi wasn't seeing the usual encouraging expression.

"Let's see here, y'all want to borrow a raft, a frame with oars, some dry bags, a cooler, a couple of tents…" Mr. Bottington checked off items on a list he was making. "You need a couple of water jugs, a first aid kit, a rescue rope, and…mmmm…you'll need a pump to take with you. You're goin' to launch from Mexican Hat instead of the upper put-in, so that makes for a shorter trip. That gets you pretty well outfitted. And as a private party, I'm sure you've already got the river permit."

Permit?

"Uh, we need a permit?" Mogi asked slowly.

"Well, sure," Mr. Bottington said in a matter-of-fact voice. "The San Juan is a regulated river since everybody and his brother wants to get on the river and play like they're in the Grand Canyon. So the Bureau of Land Management uses a permit system to control the number of people on the river at any one time."

Mogi felt his face go red. They needed to go this weekend. "Uh, how do we get a permit?"

"There's a website you go to that has an application form. Fill it out, send it with a credit card number, then they send you a permit to show the BLM river ranger whenever you launch. Easy as snow meltin' in August, provided there's a date available."

Mogi's face fell like a curtain. It wasn't going to work.

The permit, even if he could get one, would take at least a week. And he doubted they'd issue one to a bunch of teenagers, anyway.

Burl Bottington looked at the four youngsters and thought for a minute.

"This here is a three-day weekend for you guys, right?"

"That's why we have to go now," Jennifer said in a pleading voice. "If we wait for school to be out, Becky and Frank will have gone back home. We've already gotten permission from our parents and their dad, but it's because he's working overtime this whole week and wouldn't be around anyway.

"This is the only time we can all go together!"

Mr. Bottington lifted his hand to his stubbled chin

and rubbed it. His eyes took on a more serious light. He looked up at Mogi.

"You're not goin' to play with the ghosts, are ya? I hear there's been funny goin's-on, lately. Ya plannin' on doin' anythin' dangerous?"

Mogi hadn't thought about any danger in going back to the mesa. The Man in the Blue Parka surely wouldn't be there, it had been a month since the school trip. It must have been just a coincidence that they saw him then. And the bad things were happening in Bluff, not on the river.

"Nah. This is just a fun trip down the river," he tried to say with conviction.

The noise of a pickup pulling up outside interrupted the conversation. The five people around the table fell silent. A man strolled into the room.

"Howdy there, Bottington," he called out.

"Evenin' there, Bill," Mr. Bottington replied in a cool voice.

The man moved up next to Mogi. He wore brown trousers and a light green work shirt with a name across the pocket and a large badge on the sleeve reading Bureau of Land Management. The man was a river ranger for the BLM, the kind of ranger responsible for checking river permits.

"What can I do for ya, Bill?"

"Oh, just passing through. Checking the condition of the launch ramps, making sure all the right pieces of paper are up on the bulletin boards. Seems like every year we get more and more people who don't know they need permits to go rafting on the river."

As he said the last sentence, he looked directly at the four teenagers.

"It would be bad if we caught anybody launching without a permit."

Mogi now felt even worse.

"Well, I declare," Mr. Bottington said. "You're not implyin' that the honest river expedition owners and river guides are helpin' this to happen, are ya?"

His voice was even, but Mogi could hear the tone of defiance. Mr. Bottington obviously didn't like Bill.

"Oh, no, no," the man replied. "Just making an observation is all."

He shifted his eyes back to the large man at the table, gazed around the room, smirked, and wandered back toward the door.

"Well, I'd like to stay and talk more about the consequences of breaking the law, but I need to be getting on. We'll be stepping up patrols of the launch areas, by the way. See you later, Bottington." The ranger gave a small wave over his shoulder as he left, then got into his pickup and roared off.

The teenagers were silent. Burl sat with his chin propped up by his hand.

"There's just somethin' about that man I don't like," he said softly as he turned back to the list. It was about a minute before he looked up again.

"You have a dollar?"

Mogi was taken by surprise. Without asking why, he quickly reached for his billfold, took out a dollar bill, and laid it on the table.

Mr. Bottington got up and went to an old desk.

Pulling out a file drawer, he shuffled through a few folders. Finding what he wanted, he retrieved two sheets of paper and came back to the table. Taking the pen from his pocket, he placed the papers in front of Mogi.

"You can't go on the river without a permit. Sure as the world, Ranger Rick there will be watchin' for ya and would throw ya in the hoosegow if he could. I can't sell you a commercial trip on the river 'cause I ain't takin' ya. I can't rent you the equipment 'cause nobody's an adult. So I tell ya what I'm goin' to do. Providin' that you promise to row a raft as well as you did on the school trip, I'm hirin' you to do a complimentary cleanup trip of the river. The BLM won't worry about that since they encourage the outfitters to do it.

"One boat, four people, three days. I'm payin' you the handsome amount of two dollars for the trip, but since you want to take your friends along, they have to pay one dollar each for their own expenses. I owe you two, you owe me three. With your one dollar, that means we are now all paid up."

Mr. Bottington reached over, took Mogi's dollar, and put it beside him.

"Jennifer, put your Jane Henry on the bottom line there, bein' the oldest and obviously the smartest person on this expedition, and you're legal for the river. You are thereby covered by my commercial permit for river trips, about which there is no doubt, and if you are questioned by any ranger on the river, just show 'im the paperwork.

"Mogi, if you will sign the other paper, showing that you are a river guide in my employ, you're allowed to use my equipment without my supervision, and everythin' is covered by my insurance."

Jennifer quickly signed the paperwork as Mogi signed his. That done, the four teenagers drew close to the table as if discussing a secret agreement.

"Now," Mr. Bottington continued, lowering his voice and seeming to have joined the conspiracy. "Y'all need to get off as soon as you can on Friday and go as far as you can before you make camp. The river is runnin' fast, like in April, but you're still goin' to hafta row a lot to get out by Sunday evening. The good news is that fast water means there's hardly any danger from rapids, since you'll be shootin' over the rocks that would normally give you trouble.

"The only exception is Government Rapid. It's the biggest rapid on the river, the most dangerous, and worse at high water than at low. It's marked on the map, and you'll remember it when you see it. I hereby require you to carry the raft and all of your stuff around it. It's too dangerous this time of year for someone who hasn't run it before.

"I'll give you your waterproof bags right now so you can have your gear packed before you show up. Remember that your cell phones are useless in the canyons, so I wouldn't even bother taking them. I'll have the boat down at the launch site at exactly two o'clock on Friday, all set to go, so y'all be ready when you get out of school. We'll strap everythin' in and ya'll can be on your way. I'll have a truck at the Clay

Hills takeout at four o'clock on Sunday to pick you up and bring you back home. Don't be late.

"Don't worry about bein' hassled by Mr. Ranger, although I don't quite understand why he seems intent on you not goin'. He's only a part-timer and likes to have an afternoon donut with the waitress up at the coffee shop in Bluff, so I don't expect to see 'im around the two o'clock time frame."

The four teenagers were smiling. They were going to do it!

"And three more things," Mr. Bottington said as he put the pen back in his pocket. The four looked into his eyes.

"This dollar bill better not be counterfeit," he said with a small smile. "And you ought to take a couple of garbage bags and fill them up with trash you find along the river. You are workin' for me, ya know."

He then looked at them with a serious face.

"And y'all be careful. If you see somethin' stupid to do, don't do it."

They all nodded and promised that they wouldn't.

Each of them knew they had just lied.

———

It was a race when the bell rang.

Burl had the raft pumped up, framed, strapped, in the water, and ready to launch when the four conspirators pulled up in the Franklin family pickup. He added a few things to the cooler as they loaded their food from the truck and then secured it into the frame.

Frank and Mogi put the river bags behind the oarsman's seat. The red raft was outfitted with yellow oars as the cargo boat had been on the school trip. After a long, blue strap was pulled tight across the river bags, it was time to fit the ladder on.

Ladder?

Mr. Bottington decided not to ask. In his heart, he knew the teens were up to something. But kids *need* to be up to something, he thought to himself. These are good kids, so it won't be anything bad, and they're smart enough to be safe. It's an adventure. And we all could use a little adventure. If you're going to have adventure, then it should be when you're young. You get older and you get shy about things like that.

Mr. Bottington watched the four friends struggle to tie on the twenty-four-foot extension ladder from the Franklin garage, finally surrendering to the reality that one end had to be shoved almost back to where Mogi sat and tied onto the front seat and front tube, with the other end hanging out almost ten feet beyond the front of the boat.

The passengers had to cram in around it, the raft was harder to row, and it looked really dumb besides, like a silver battering ram on the front of a big inner tube.

"I've seen Mogi row before, so the rest of you better be on your toes," he cautioned the teenagers with a smile. "And don't be runnin' into rocks, ya got me?"

Mogi grinned. He had loved rowing on the school trip, and even Mr. Bottington said he was a natural. It would be easy!

The four teenagers buckled on their PFDs. Once more, Mr. Bottington went through an equipment check-list with them, told them what to do in an emergency, and reminded them of the rules of river safety.

He looked into the eyes of each of them as he talked about safety. There was a lot that could happen on a river.

Flexing his large arms as he gave the raft a hefty shove, Burl Bottington pushed them off from the shore. Mogi lowered the oars and, after fumbling for a few seconds, moved them into the current with a few strong strokes.

They all gave a final wave to the big man on the shore and then focused on the river ahead of them—not seeing the usual grin leave Burl Bottington's face.

He was worried. Maybe he should have made them spill the beans. He had trusted his intuition to let them go but now was having second thoughts. There was something in Jennifer's eyes that looked like a plea for help.

And then there was that ladder...

———

On the rugged, mostly naked countryside a couple of hundred yards above the drifting raft, the village of Mexican Hat snoozed through another afternoon.

The curves of the San Juan River defined the shape of the town, and a solitary bridge on the west end took Highway 163, the only wholly paved road in Mexican Hat, from one side of the river to the other. From the nearby covered patio of an ancient but always-filled motel on a cliff above the river, several generations of tourists had watched rafting groups drift under the bridge and wondered what was around the next bend in the river.

It was still early in the rafting season, but the motel was full from the busloads of tourists coming from or headed to Monument Valley, its rock formations made famous by photographs and movies less than twenty miles away.

The motel's front desk cashier, though usually busy with customers, routinely kept watch on the river for rafts floating by.

As the four explorers and their battering ram swept past the motel's bank of windows, the cashier gazed down at the odd-looking arrangement with a confused look. After they passed, she searched the corkboard above the counter, found the thumbtacked business card the stranger had given her, picked up the phone, and called the number.

After all, the man had paid her in advance.

Someone answered, and she spoke slowly: "One raft, four teenagers, an extension ladder.

"Ya have any idea what the ladder is for?" the woman asked.

"Thank you," the man said and hung up.

CHAPTER 13

After the time spent in anxious waiting, the four teenagers had been eager for the river to carry them to the mesa and the mysterious opening in its wall.

Now, watching the bridge disappear around a bend in the river behind them, the adventurers were completely on their own, and they were afraid.

Between the bridge and the take-out some sixty miles away, there were no roads, no trails, no way to get from the river to the rocky rim a thousand or more feet above them, no telephones, no cell phones, no houses, no people for help. They could not turn back, and they could not avoid what lay ahead. On the school trip, no one had thought twice about danger. Worry belonged to the adults, and they never seemed worried at all. Now there were no adults, and the loneliness of the river began to sit on their shoulders.

If they found the opening, what about The Man in the Blue Parka? No matter how many times Mogi assured them it was only a coincidence that the man was at the opening the last time, the others did not believe it. No one talked about it, but everyone thought it: What would they do if he was still there? What would he do if he found them?

Mogi focused on his rowing, keeping the raft in the current as much as possible, making long, smooth strokes, urging the boat forward. It was a lot tougher with the ladder sticking so far out, changing how the raft behaved, making it harder to turn and to avoid the shore, and he kept banging his hands against the metal.

But he knew he had to keep rowing, that they needed to hurry. His muscles were tense, and several times over the next three hours, Mogi rubbed his biceps and stretched his back. Every now and then, he fingered his chest wound. The itch was bad, but it was the slow, continuous burn of the muscles that bothered him most.

Rowing a raft was exactly what he shouldn't be doing.

The three others had offered to row, but Mogi just couldn't let the oars go. He remembered the difficulty he'd had when Mr. Bottington first let him row— needing his long arms to get leverage on the long oars, maneuvering from one side of the river to the other, watching the current and knowing when to turn or rotate. It was hard, and the ladder made everything ten times worse. It wasn't the time for Frank and Becky to learn, and Jennifer couldn't row as fast as he could.

It was his curiosity that got them here, and his plan that would get them down the river with enough time to get everything done.

"You're bleeding," Jennifer said, pointing at his chest.

Mogi looked down and saw a dark spot below the bandage. More than likely, he'd pulled out a stitch.

He looked at his sister and shrugged. What could he do? Put a Band-Aid on it from the first aid kit? He knew he couldn't stop the movement that would keep the wound open. Hopefully, it wouldn't get worse.

Becky stared at the river canyon ahead, thinking. She felt the polished piece of turquoise in her pocket and said her wish all over again. Could it come true? She didn't think so, but a deep belief inside her refused to leave. If there was any chance—any at all— she and Frank had to find out.

More of this stone and her father could go back to his work. More of this stone and the Nation's spirit could be restored. The thought invaded her dreams at night.

Would they find a new source of the precious rock on the San Juan?

Wouldn't it be something if they had their own source of good stone? She knew it would bring more spirit to their rituals, more power to their chants. Everyone who had it would be stronger.

It wouldn't be just turquoise, it would be Navajo turquoise.

Would the spirits of the river lead her to it?

Jennifer felt cold, but she knew it wasn't from the air.

She was scared. Lying awake the night before, she wondered about the man whose eyes looked back at her from the photograph.

Four men had disappeared on this river almost sixty years before she was born. Mogi was right, she thought.

It's all mixed together—the old mystery, the new happenings. But being mixed together brought only more questions that had no answers.

Frank was quiet, as usual. His gaze went from the water to the rocks to the vegetation to the sky. It was the land of The People. He had no fear of the land. He wasn't sure what lay ahead, but curiosity was part of the wonder of life, and life would accommodate it. Whatever the four of them sought, it would be found. He could wait. The important thing was to stay balanced, be ready to receive what the day brought.

As the sun moved toward its late afternoon position, the raft's progress along the river felt incredibly slow, pulling the teens' spirits down, giving time for their inner fears to grow.

After what seemed like more hours than they could count, the stranded mesa came into view. As they pulled into shore, shadows from the cliffs covered the campsite.

The last rays of sunlight, soft and muted, were high against the canyon walls.

Tying the raft to a boulder, they hurried up the draw.

They couldn't wait, even knowing it would be hard to see details in the dim light. Climbing to where Mogi and Frank had hid from the rainstorm and even farther up to see the opening more clearly, they kept looking over their shoulders.

And saw nothing. Even with binoculars, no man, no cave, no opening was visible. Nothing but blank sandstone.

Mogi felt sick. What if he had been wrong about everything? What if the dark slit was only a shadow?

They walked back, following the beams of their flashlights.

———

"Maybe the man was a skinwalker who wanted you to come back," Frank said, watching the embers glow as the campfire burned to coals. "Maybe that's why you couldn't find any tracks farther up the canyon. He'd changed into a raven or something."

"I used to think you were crazy to believe in skin-walkers," Mogi said as he stirred the coals with a stick. "It doesn't seem so strange now. This country, uh, well, there's just something weird about it."

"It has a spirit of its own," Jennifer said, surprising the others. "I'm not exactly a lightning rod for strikes of the supernatural, but there's something here, some-thing about the whole place, maybe the oldness of everything. I feel..." She struggled with the words. "...like, squeezed by everything around me."

Squeezed. Mogi liked the word. Yeah, everything

around him—the rocks, the river, the stories, the mysteries, the loneliness—they were squeezing him too.

"Do Navajo go to church?" Jennifer asked, putting another stick on the fire and blowing the coals. She didn't want to go to bed, either because she wasn't sleepy or out of fear—she wasn't sure which. What if the thief in the night came back?

"Not the way you think," Becky answered. "Traditionally, we get together as family and as little groups, but it usually has a specific purpose, like a new baby, or a healing, or a cleansing ceremony. Sometimes there are big gatherings, like powwows or market days. The idea of getting together for religion, though, is not the same as yours.

"We see every day as part of life. Being part of the Spirit is who we are and what we do. It's not separate."

Alternating stories, the reservation twins talked about their Navajo beliefs. There were stories about different worlds that existed, about First Man and First Woman, Navajo deities singing beauty and life into being, giving outer forms to the sun, the moon, dawn, twilight, sky, darkness, fire, water, hills, rocks, springs, rivers, and inner forms as well, singing the essence of vibrant life into every person.

"It is very important to us that we live our lives in *hozho*," Frank said, "with harmony and peace. The world was created for us, and we are to be in harmony with it.

"You guys have good and evil. We have *hozho* and disorder.

"When we lose harmony with everything around us, we feel out of place, disturbed, out of balance. A lot of our ceremonies are meant to rid us of whatever is causing the disharmony and return us to peace."

Becky went on with more of the Navajo story. Jennifer was absorbed in what she said, but Mogi couldn't take it all in. It didn't sound logical. There were lots of references to monsters and other creatures, to alien gods, to babies being born out of rainbows, lightning, and clouds. There were twins named Monster Slayer and Born for Water. And someone named Spider Woman, who gave Monster Slayer the weapons to destroy monsters.

Mogi was pretty sure he'd never heard any of his ministers talk about stuff like that.

The fire lit up in a last blaze, dimmed into the soft glow of tiny ingots of gold, and then was gone.

―――――

The four friends started before sunrise because three of them had not gotten a wink of sleep. Frank slept like a log.

"Let's get everything packed into the raft and ready to go," Mogi suggested. "Then we can use all of our time to explore."

"How long do you think we'll be?" Jennifer asked.

"I don't know. I don't know what we're going to find."

Walking up the draw and leaving the ladder at the bottom, they went up the side of the canyon where they had gone after leaving the raft.

"Unbelievable," Mogi said as he passed the binoculars to the others seated along the sloping side of the canyon.

At the ledge where the man had stood, the ledge they had focused on the night before, there was now an opening in the face of the rock. Directly above where the waterfall had been, the black opening stood out against the tan of the sunlit rock.

The four discussed where the ladder should be placed to reach each of the ledges—one, two, three, four climbs—until they were finally satisfied with the route.

Mogi jumped up and started back to the ladder.

Frank waited as the others started down to the draw, keeping his seat with the binoculars trained at the canyon wall, looking back and forth, looking for what, he wasn't sure. Finally he lowered them and stood up. Mogi was calling.

Starting down the canyon side, he moved uneasily, a strong fear hounding him from the back of his mind.

"No way that opening was there last night," Frank muttered to himself. "It was opened just for us."

CHAPTER 14

"It's a good thing we brought the twenty-four footer," Mogi said as he helped Becky onto the flat part of the last ledge. It had taken all of the ladder's length to make the final climb.

"Did you find it?" he called behind him. Jennifer and Frank had already walked across the ledge.

"I don't understand this at all," he heard Jennifer say.

When he and Becky went over to where she was standing, he understood her reaction.

It was a natural opening of a tunnel, maybe two and a half feet wide and three feet high, a hole obviously carved by years of erosion. A well-worn depression in the rock led from the bottom of the opening over to the edge of the cliff, where it would have been the top of the waterfall.

But around the outside of the opening, a sharp lip had been cut into the rock with some kind of saw.

Inside the opening, a series of metal brackets were bolted into the rock.

Frank knelt down and touched them, looking at how they were positioned around the opening. He rocked back on his heels. Looking around on the ground to the side of the tunnel opening, he spied what he expected to find.

"Check that out," he said as he pointed.

It was a flat, thin piece of rock about the size of the opening. In fact, exactly the size of the opening. It didn't take much imagination to see that it fit the shape of the carved lip. If it was set directly into the opening, it would fit like the cover on a manhole.

Mogi and Frank pulled the cover into an upright position. On the back, a series of rods had been attached that matched the brackets in the opening.

When rotated by a lever on the inside or by some tool stuck in a little hole in the outside, the rods locked into the brackets attached to the opening in the ledge's wall.

The bottom part of the door had an opening about a foot wide by six inches high to allow water from inside the tunnel to flow out.

"This is solid rock, shaped to fit the opening exactly," Mogi said. "When it's in place, I bet you can't tell there's an opening at all."

"That's why we didn't see it last night," Frank added.

"The cover was in place. Which means..." he trailed off, raising his eyes to the others.

"What it means," Becky said, "is that someone's expecting us. We've been invited to come in."

"I don't like this at all, Mogi," Jennifer was the first to say. "This is not right. We're in the middle of absolutely nowhere, and suddenly, we've got a hidden tunnel and somebody's waiting for us. I think we're in over our heads, and we ought to get out of here. Now! We'll report this to the sheriff when we get back and let him investigate."

"Now, hold on. Let's not get overly excited," Mogi said.

"We don't know anything for sure."

"Know anything? What do you want, a signed invitation? We were coming to check this out, but we all agreed that there was no way that anybody was still going to be here, remember? Well, there *is* somebody here, and we need to get back in that raft right now!'

"Okay, well, let's just think a minute about it, okay?"

Mogi asked. It wasn't what he'd expected either. Maybe a cave, but not a tunnel with a custom door.

What in the world was going on?

Becky and Frank were scared and didn't mind saying so, but were even more curious. They had grown up close to the land, this vast area of thousands of square miles. It was home, the land of their people. It had always been a land of surprises and unexpected events, and they sensed no automatic evil. Real ghosts wouldn't have bothered to build nicely engineered doors.

And something else also was driving the brother

and sister—something they had to find out. It could mean a return of the spirit to The People. If there was any chance at all, they had to take the risk.

Mogi finally responded.

"We don't know what this is. We don't know what it means. We've been careful up until now, and we'll always be able to come back out if we need to. And there's no way for this door to pick itself up and close behind us.

"I think we need to check it out just a little further. I'll go inside. If it looks like a bad thing, I'll come right out.

"If everything looks okay, then we'll all go inside. Would that work for everyone?"

Jennifer wasn't convinced, and it took a few more assurances from her brother, with the help of Becky and Frank, to get her agreement. They all got out their flashlights. Then Mogi took a deep breath, squatted down, and crawled through the opening.

It was surprisingly smooth. Moving on his knees, he took his time to look at how the tunnel had been made, as if high-quality engineering would reflect a friendlier builder. Soon he was able to stand up in the tunnel.

Everything looked fine.

Mogi called to the others, and was soon joined by Jennifer and Becky. Frank was last, moving more slowly.

Flashing his light around, Mogi continued along the passageway.

Sometimes the tunnel was tall and narrow, sometimes short and wide, but the ceiling was always higher than their heads. Every wall was scarred by hammer marks.

This tunnel was no accident. It was well-traveled and well-maintained.

Mogi relaxed. There didn't seem to be any danger after all.

"Mogi," Frank whispered after they'd gone about thirty feet. "Listen!"

He stopped and turned. The loudest sound was his heartbeat and breathing. Straining, he could barely make out sounds from the ledge outside the tunnel: boots crunching gravel, a short, deep thump, then a screech, sharp as a knife, as if metal bars were rotating into their brackets.

Jennifer started shaking all over, and four sets of eyes grew to silver dollar size.

Someone had closed and bolted the door.

CHAPTER 15

INSIDE THE STRANDED MESA, APRIL 1934

The tunnel to the outside continued to spew a cloud of dust at the four men. They had no doubt. The lightning, the shaking of the rocks, and the billowing dust made it clear that the tunnel opening was now blocked.

J.D. and Little Jake scrambled away from the entrance and started cursing their luck. Navajo Bob slid even closer to the wall, leaving Kattrick lying alone next to the shallow pool, hacking and coughing, struggling to catch his breath.

As his coughing gradually subsided, Kattrick pulled himself upright.

"Shut up, all of you," he bellowed. "We've got to think, so shut up, shut up now!" He glared at the others. "Does anybody remember any other entrance, any other tunnel that wasn't explored? For God's sake, does anybody remember another way out of here?"

No one answered.

Kattrick's fear changed to anger. He spat, turned, and bitterly climbed to the upper level.

J.D. and Little Jake started checking the bottom reaches of the labyrinth again, hoping for a passage they'd missed.

They found nothing. Bob remained sitting alone, chanting under his breath, accepting his death.

When they got back, Kattrick told J.D. and Little Jake to help him carry all the gear and equipment to the top floor. They couldn't figure out why but feared their boss's temper too much to ask. Up and down, up and down, the three men carried food, blankets, clothes, maps, rock hammers, even a roll of yellow measuring string on a metal reel. Kattrick wanted it all moved.

Going over the equipment, cursing himself for leaving the ropes hanging on the ledges of the mesa, he knew that the only way out was the obvious one.

The opening in the roof.

The slit in the rock ceiling was about a hundred feet long. Part of it was as close as twenty feet from the upper floor. The mesa top seemed split in half, each side forming an overhanging layer of rock that almost met in the middle. The long opening between them arched over the emptiness above the chamber's pools.

If there were some way to get a rope through the

opening, someone could climb out and get help. But rope was the one thing they didn't have.

For three days, the fearful men were like prison cellmates who hated each other. Kattrick rationed the amount of food and when they could have it. When J.D. rebelled on the third day and tried to eat everything he could get his hands on, Kattrick beat him until the other men pulled him off. Little food was left.

Feeling crushed by the boredom, with only his fear to think about, the geologist in him drove Kattrick back to the vent pipe, chipping away, still looking for more stones.

Eventually, he gave up and just kept walking around the chambers, trying to sweat away his nerves but failing. Bob was the calmest one, sitting back against a rock wall on the bottom level, avoiding the others, silent.

It was Little Jake who decided he wasn't going to die.

Though most of the slit loomed directly over the empty space at the center of the cavern, one end overlapped a section of the top shelf so that Jake could look straight up between the rock layers. He couldn't see the sky, but he knew it was close on the other side.

Taking the blankets from their makeshift beds, he cut narrow strips of cloth and braided them around each other into a rough rope. Then he put the four rock hammers together, sharp points out, and tied them together with the yellow measuring line to make a grappling hook.

Tying the line holding the hammers to the blanket rope gave him almost forty feet of rope and hook.

Kattrick and J.D. watched. Little Jake was stupid, so they didn't expect success. Still, as the rope grew, it occurred to them that his idea just might work.

Jake moved below the slit, started swinging, and let the grappling hook fly at the height of his swing.

He missed.

Over and over again, Little Jake, then J.D., then Kattrick tried their best at swinging the hammers in a circular motion and letting go at the precise time to go through the opening.

They never even got close.

The others gave up in frustration and went back to sulking, but Little Jake didn't quit. Time and time again, he tried to get the hammers through the slit. Time and time again, he failed.

Resting from his efforts, he had a new idea. He unwrapped the hammer combination and rewound it with only two hammers. There was less hook but also half the weight.

Time and time again, he tried.

But with this combination, he got better.

Cutting the weight in half made the difference. Little Jake could get the combination up into the slit about every third time he threw. All he needed was to swing faster, giving it more energy to go beyond the slit and out—hopefully into rocks on the mesa top.

The others had begun to notice as he started hitting the slit. Watching, surprised, hoping beyond belief, they began to cheer him on.

But he didn't have the arm for it.

J.D. tried and got closer, once getting the hook about five feet past the opening. But when he gave it a little tug, the grapple slid on the smooth sandstone outside and fell back through the slit. Gathering the cloth rope for another try, Little Jake noticed the frayed ends. If it was going to work, it would have to be soon.

"Let me try," a voice said. It was Navajo Bob.

Raised on the back of a pony on the reservation, he understood the finesse required to drop a noose around the neck of a running horse. He gathered the funny-feeling rope in his left hand and started swinging the grapple over his head with his right. Slowly, evenly, he let more rope through his hand, feeding it into an ever-increasing circle, letting the swinging rope dip into the emptiness of the rock overhangs below. Faster and faster, he moved his whole body with the rope.

Bob made two more full revolutions. In the last half revolution, they could see him putting his whole upper body into whipping the hook through the air. Raising his arm at the last moment, leaning his body back against the force, swishing the hook into a raised arc, he let the rope go.

The hammers sailed through the slit without touching the sides. It seemed as if they must have flown a full fifteen feet beyond the edge. The men in the cave heard a distant clink and clank as the hook landed.

"Careful, now," Kattrick cautioned as Navajo Bob,

holding tight on the cloth rope, sweating with concentration, gently pulled. The men could hear the hammers dragging across the ground.

The rope stopped. Navajo Bob slowly applied more force. It didn't move. He pulled harder. It still didn't move.

With the utmost care, he pulled on the rope with all his strength.

A cry of relief went out from everyone—a frenzy of emotion and pent-up feelings. Dancing and shouting, they looked like a house of crazy men. "We did it! We did it!" J.D. kept yelling.

Who's idea was it? Little Jake remembered, with the tiniest smile at what he knew was to come. The smallest and lightest, he was the obvious choice to go up the rope.

Then he could use the woven rope to let himself down the side of the mesa to where the climbing ropes had been left. He should clear away the rocks from the opening if he could. If he couldn't, he should take a boat to go for help. It might be two or three days, but he'd be back to get them.

Giving him a few tins of food, the three others watched Little Jake carefully climb the rope, hand over hand, and maneuver through the slit.

"I'm going next," J.D. cried as he seized hold of the hanging end. He gripped it with both hands as high as he could reach, jumped up to hold it with his feet, then moved his hands higher.

He strained to lift himself, but his body didn't move.

"Don't," Little Jake shouted down. "Stop! You're pulling the hammers out of the rock."

Kattrick grabbed at J.D.'s shoulders and pulled him off the rope. "He needs it!" Kattrick yelled. "He has to get to the ledge where the ropes are."

Little Jake began pulling it up. The men below stopped breathing as they watched the rope disappear. It had been their only hope of escape, the symbol of their rescue.

Now that it was gone, their hope was Jake.

Outside, he used the blanket rope to work his way down to the ledge where the tunnel began, then used the other ropes there to get to the bottom.

Hitting the dry riverbed at the foot of the mesa, happily hiking the short distance back to the boats, he devoured the food the others had given him and threw the empty tins in the river. The boats were heavy and hard to pull down to the water. Once he had done it, Jake erased the drag marks, looked over the area to make sure no signs of the four men were left, then tied the second boat to the first and shoved off.

When he felt far enough from the stranded mesa that no one would connect it with anything found sunken there, he pulled the second boat into shallow water and bashed holes in the side and bottom. He struggled to get it back in the current where the water could flow in, but the boat had been built to be almost unsinkable. Finally, he gave up, pushed it as far into the current as he could, and let it go.

Taking the other boat, Jake floated past the usual

takeout place, on through the canyons that would someday be covered by Lake Powell, and stopped a short distance above a small village near the Arizona border, hiding close to the bank until after dark. Aiming to be more successful this time, he bashed four holes in the bottom of the boat and weighted it down with the biggest rocks he could handle, then moved it toward the middle of the river as it sank below the surface. A few years of silt and it will be a fossil before anyone sees it again, he joked to himself.

Jake took another look by moonlight at the rocks he'd taken from the jar and put in his pocket without anyone noticing back at the mesa. Green, blue, red— he didn't know how much they'd be worth, but the geologist had obviously thought they'd be worth something.

When the stones had all been sold, he could always go back, dig out the entrance tunnel or drop through the top, and get more. And maybe a few pots while he was at it.

It was too bad about the others. What a lousy way to die.

Oh, well, that's life, Jake told himself as he trotted along the shoreline, circling to find a road and walking into the village from the reservation side. Coming in on foot, he'd never be connected with the river.

He'd be just another drifter on his way to somewhere else.

CHAPTER 16

INSIDE THE MESA, TODAY

With the clank of the rock door's metal latches slamming into their brackets, all the positive strength Mogi had had on the ledge outside evaporated. He had made a serious mistake. He had led them into a trap.

Mogi flicked off his flashlight and motioned for Frank to do the same. If someone had come into the tunnel after them, he wanted to see their light first.

"Mogi! What are we going to do?" Jennifer screamed in the softest whisper she could.

"Shhhh!"

He peered into the darkness behind them for a few seconds. No sounds. No lights. Nothing.

"I don't hear anybody," he said quietly to Frank. The four pressed close together.

It was a horror story coming true—trapped in a

tunnel by an unknown creature, any retreat shut off forever.

Mogi turned his light on and stood listening to the breathing of those around him. The closeness of the tunnel walls, the flashlight beams bouncing nervously around the room, the darkness beyond them—all made it as frightening as anything he had ever felt in his life.

Haltingly, unsure of himself, he moved and put his arms around Jennifer. He leaned his cheek down on her head and felt her on the edge of a scream. Becky put her arms around them both, and Frank joined the embrace. Each of them was quivering, and Mogi knew he was too. From his head to his toes.

It was a full minute before he wanted to—before he could—break away.

"We'll make it through," he said as he let go. "We'll make it through."

The shutting of the tunnel door meant someone had gotten to the ledge in the few short minutes they had been in the tunnel. Whoever they were dealing with was clever and awfully quick. And he must know their every move.

Shining his light ahead, then to the side, then back, then ahead, half-seeing, half-feeling his way along the tunnel, Mogi inched forward, straining to see and hear as much as he could. A few curves, and he saw a dim light ahead of him.

He stopped and pointed. The others followed his finger to where the tunnel floor rose steeply, then became a set of narrow metal stair-steps bolted into the sandstone.

Mogi carefully, silently, went up. Cautiously reaching the opening above him and peering over the edge, he stepped up into a large room. He crouched quietly as the others came up and moved next to him. Slowly, they stood up and stepped forward until they stood on the solid rock in front of the stairway.

They were in a large cave stretching far overhead until it met some kind of opening at the top. A metal stairway in front of them led up a dozen feet or so to another level, and other stairs led up to other sections farther away. The huge room was motionless, full of deadly quiet, like a funeral, with a stink of wet, rusted metal.

No one could be seen. Light bulbs burned in fixtures at the top of each section of the stairway.

"What in the world is this?" Jennifer whispered as the four teens crowded together in dumbfounded silence.

Mogi could only shake his head. Not a clue.

It seemed only natural to follow the stairs, so he did, slowly, carefully, as quietly as he could, with Jennifer holding onto the straps of his daypack. The twins followed close behind. As Mogi moved higher, he saw pools of water on the sandstone floors near the bottom of each stairway.

At the top level, the lone bulb was on but sent little light into the recesses of the room. Mogi looked up for the first time at the long slit of daylight in the rock ceiling above them.

Jennifer tugged on his straps and pointed ahead.

"What in the world…? Are those petroglyphs?"

Jennifer and Mogi walked forward to get a closer look.

It seemed to be a ring of graffiti, meaningless and childish drawings on the wall all around the room. Some were playful figures from comic books or newspapers or writings meant to be funny or crude. But when Mogi and Jennifer moved closer, they could see even in the dim light that the graffiti had been scrawled on top of a huge panel of Anasazi symbols—rock carvings that extended from the floor to the ceiling in places. Mogi could make out deer symbols, spirals, shadow pictures of hands, maybe corn and snakes.

Whatever they were, they had been recklessly defaced.

He noticed that Becky and Frank had not moved from the stairway and walked back to them.

"You worried about spirits?"

Frank looked at Becky and then at Mogi.

"It's not the rock carvings," he said. "This is a bad place. There is evil here." His eyes looked directly into Mogi's. "We need to get out of here as soon as we can."

Becky let out a small scream.

Twenty feet away, to the left of the drawings on the wall, next to a long wooden table, a man was sitting in a chair.

The others jumped at the scream and hurried to her side as she pointed. They froze, afraid to speak.

"I suppose we ought to introduce each other," the

man said, "but that seems to be such a shallow way of starting a relationship." His voice was high and thin, his words followed by a long laugh. "Anyway, I really don't care who you are, and I certainly don't want to know your names. It might give me bad dreams or something," the voice cackled again. The laugh was a little wilder.

"I am so funny! Don't you think so? Oh, I suppose not." The voice didn't seem real. "You probably don't understand a single thing about what's going on here, and you're dying to know who I am and how I got here and have just one question after another!"

The man stood up and casually tossed four sets of handcuffs onto the rock floor in front of them. "Put these on," he said, laughing as if it was a theatrical performance.

Mogi, jolted from being dumbfounded, responded with what he thought was a reasonable statement.

"You've got to be nuts if you think I'm putting those on."

The man's quickness was remarkable. In a split second, the barrel of a pistol was pointed at the center of Mogi's forehead.

"Go ahead, punk, make my day!" he said. His laugh rose in pitch—almost hysterically—as he swung the pistol from one side of Mogi's face to the other.

"Oh, all right, we should do this correctly. Every-body turn around," the man said, waving the gun in front of their faces, "and I'll play Texas Ranger."

He was rough, twisting their wrists, making the cuffs too tight. With their hands behind them, the man turned them around and shoved them hard into a kneeling position.

Mogi, confused, bewildered, and scared out of his wits, tried to focus on the man in front of him. Maybe fifty. Tall, slightly built, almost bald. At least two inches taller than Mogi. Wearing dusty jeans and a work shirt.

And work boots.

The man moved in front of them. "I hope you kids appreciate my engineering. It was no mean trick getting everything to fit so well you couldn't see the seams. And my second tunnel on that ledge. You missed it completely. That's how I could lock you in and get here in time to greet you with open arms."

The man cackled. Then he looked more closely at Frank and Becky. "Oh, my goodness," he exclaimed.

"What do we have here? Oh, my goodness, we have Indians! Oh, please, please, please—can I have my picture taken with you?" The man roared again with a high-pitched cackle. He got his chair and put it in front of them. But instead of sitting in it, he just paced back and forth behind it, crossing and recrossing the sandstone floor as if it were a stage.

"Oh, how shall I begin," he started, laying his forearm across his forehead, feigning indecision. "Oh, okay, if it has to be at the beginning, then it will have to do!

"I'm the ghost of the San Juan," the man said in a hysterical voice, then laughed the maniacal laugh again.

"Well, if you have to have the truth, I'm only one of

the ghosts of the San Juan. Okay, okay, okay—you've probably guessed that I'm lying a teeny-weeny bit.

"I'm actually the grandson of one of the ghosts of the San Juan."

CHAPTER 17

W   ith the overacting of a vaudeville
        performer, interrupting himself with
        bursts of high-pitched laughter, the man
told a fascinating story.

In 1933, a geologist doing mapping for an oil
company found several gemstones in a place they
should not have been, in a catch basin in a dry
riverbed surrounding a stranded mesa on the San
Juan River. He kept his discovery secret and came
back a year later with three men he'd hired in
Mexican Hat, hoping to find the source of the gems.

"What they discovered was this," the man said,
sweeping his hand over the whole area. "A huge
cavern hollowed out by thousands of years of rainwater coming in through a crack in the ceiling."

The men also found the source of the gemstones,
he told the four captives—a vent pipe that had
bubbled into the mesa but not broken through the
surface. The stranded mesa, the cavern, the vent pipe

—altogether, the whole thing was a fluke, a geological mistake.

"But a really, really, oh so bad thing happened. A bolt of lightning from a thunderstorm struck the rim of the mesa while they were in here, causing a landslide that covered the entrance, the very entrance that you trespassers came through a short time ago. With the only way out blocked, all of those poor explorers died a really sad death," the man said as he wiped his eyes, pretending to weep. He tilted his head to the side and looked at them with a wink.

"Uh, except for one. My grandfather."

"Your grandfather was Gordon Kattrick, the geologist," Mogi blurted out.

The tall man laughed.

"I beg your pardon! Kattrick was an idiot, like you.

"My grandfather was the runt of the expedition, the fool that everybody picked on. The stupid one. But he was the only one clever enough to find a way out. And fortunately for me, smart enough to let his companions die at the same time.

"And, by the way, smart enough to take the gemstones they had found. He was able to use some natural marketing talent—and some talent for illegal things as well—to turn them into considerable wealth by buying and selling gems all over the world. He didn't come back here for years, and when he did, it was mainly out of curiosity about what the passing of time had done to the cavern.

"When he did, he took a few more stones, but it was too much work. He never came back again. On his deathbed, he confessed to his son the story of the discovery and the fate of the other men. His son, a good manager of the gemstone wealth, was not much interested in risking the discovery of the place or the crime, so he did nothing about it.

"But my grandfather also told his grandson, who was much more interested."

The man kept walking side-to-side in front of his captive audience.

"And that was me, my grandfather's very own pride and joy and chip off the old block!" he boasted. "Yes, I've definitely increased the family wealth.

"But..." The man winked and swelled his chest. "Oh, the pain of the truth—I just want more, more, more!

"And to think, all of the future wealth of my father and grandfather started with those little red and green rocks."

"Don't forget about the diamonds," Mogi blurted out, anxious to make up for guessing wrong about who the man's grandfather was.

The tall man looked genuinely surprised and more than a little irritated at the interruption of his performance. He moved in front of Mogi.

"Well, at least you're a bright idiot. I would be fascinated to know how you knew that."

Leaning down, he looked Mogi in the eyes and then moved his gaze to the blood stain on Mogi's T-shirt from rowing the day before. The man reached down and jammed his finger hard into the stain. Mogi winced in pain.

"Oh," the man said slowly, "we meet again. I didn't have a chance to introduce myself." The man raised his arm and fiercely backhanded Mogi across the mouth.

Mogi's head jerked in a twist, and he felt his neck muscles strain from the blow.

"I believe you have been the source of all of my problems lately. I want you to know that I do not appreciate your curiosity. I'll enjoy making you suffer a little bit more than your friends."

The words were spat in Mogi's face, the voice filled with threat and menace. This man is the devil himself, Mogi thought, dribbling blood from his mouth, still wincing from the pain.

The man returned to his stage—and his history lesson.

"In spite of what our brilliant little boy has figured out, we've only gotten three diamonds out of the whole place, and they were too small to be worth the effort. It didn't really matter, though. The other stones were enough to make the business. My father and grandfather saw this place as only an interesting mistake of nature, a family secret, nothing to be made much of.

"I, on the other hand, found something that made my dreams much bigger than theirs."

The man moved to one of the tables, grabbed a rock the size of a softball, and came back in front of the four youths. It was a larger version of the chalky blue rock Mr. Jennings had handed Becky in the classroom.

"Do you recognize this, boys and girls?" He moved the rock slowly in front of them.

"Ah, I see the light in our Indian maiden!" he said as Becky's eyes grew wide with recognition. She shot a look at Frank.

"Turquoise," the man said. "My father and grandfather never realized what a fluke this place really was. I know the chemistry, but I won't bore you. Let's leave it with the idea that the lava brought up its usual mixture of minerals and crammed them into the sandstone of the mesa.

"Conveniently, the water that is so scarce in the rest of this rotten country was abundant in this cavern, where it slowly dripped, dripped, dripped for a few thousand years, dissolving the lava and other rocks into this great little mixture of phosphorus, copper, and gold.

"Seeping into the cracks surrounding the pipe, the biggest vein of turquoise I've ever seen was formed. It's taken years of work, but now I have a warehouse full of this pretty little rock.

"And you know what that means?" he said in a mocking talk show host voice as he leaned over Frank, who turned his face away in disgust.

"Oops! Wrong! Buzz, buzz, buzz. Wrong answer! You thought it meant money!"

The man suddenly grew still and serious. He moved the chair in front of them and sat down. The change in his face was clear. He no longer looked crazy, only evil.

"What it means is power. I have the largest

collection of natural, high-quality turquoise in the country. Most U.S. mines with high-quality turquoise ran dry years ago, and the few mines still producing have been bought in the last few years by two gemstone companies secretly owned by me. We've been steadily decreasing their output for years.

"But I believe I've starved the market enough now that the Navajo will do anything to regain their jewelry business."

"You..." Jennifer blurted out in shock. "You made the turquoise disappear! You're responsible for Becky's dad leaving the reservation!"

"Ah, he must be the father of these fine children.

"Whoops, looks like I'm guilty. That is *exactly* why I bought all the mines I could." Then, like a switch being flipped, the man turned to the tone of a thoughtful businessman: "It wouldn't do any good to only have part of the market.

"You see, I have enough money that there'd be only a little bit of gain from being a wealthy turquoise merchant. What I really want is to increase my wealth a big bit.

"Whole bunches, in fact.

"That's why turquoise represents not money but power.

"Who wants turquoise? Native Americans. What Native American tribe is most identified with turquoise and turquoise jewelry? The Navajo. What would the Navajo do if they were offered really good turquoise that came from the Southwest instead of some other country? Anything. And what do the Navajo have more of than any other tribe?"

The excitement in the man's eyes made them sparkle.

The four teenagers sat in silence, hating the game that was being played.

"Oh, come, come, children! This is not a hard question.

"The Navajo Nation owns what that other state entities don't?"

It was Frank who answered. His voice was as cold as ice.

"Land."

"Well, that's pretty close."

"Casinos."

"Bingo! Give that boy a prize! Of course, a lot of other tribes have casinos, but right now, my biggest advantage is with the Navajo Nation: I have something they want, and they have something I want—a share of the business. That's where the really big money is. Now, mind you, I don't actually want to do any work, like be a manager or owner who has to go to meetings and all that. I just want to be a silent partner. And the more they pay me, the more silent I will be.

"And, along the way, they get some turquoise. Not all at once, of course. I like to keep my customers hungry."

The man's voice had almost gone breathless with the excitement of his vision. Mogi was stunned by the manipulation that the idea involved.

"The Navajo will never deal with scum like you," Frank said defiantly.

"Oh, I believe they will. I'll be able to make them a deal they can't refuse. They won't mind in the beginning because the tradeoff will be good. They may regret it later when I start asking for more, but by then, it will be too late. I will have sucked them in."

The man put the turquoise back on the table and walked over to his prisoners.

"Everything was going so well until, let's see," he moved in front of Mogi, leaned forward, and poked his finger hard into the bloodstain again. "I believe it was *you* who spoiled everything."

"You were at the top of the waterfall," Mogi said angrily as he clenched his teeth from the pain stabbing his chest.

"A mistake on my part," the man said with a serious voice. "I'd been cleaning and sacking stones next to the bottom pool. I always throw the waste in the water for the summer rains to wash out. But this time, the storm came and washed away the good stones that I'd just cleaned and had ready to sack. I couldn't do anything to save them. I was outside taking a break, and I got stuck on that ledge until the water coming out the tunnel slowed enough so I could come back in.

"I watched you at the pool below as I waited.

"When I saw the good stones had been washed away too, that's when I remembered you. You'd probably found good stuff in that pool, and I knew that if you showed up with rare gemstones back at school, somebody was going to be very interested and would come looking. And that would not be good.

"Since the original expedition, there's only been my father, me, a few workers—most of whom have mysteriously died—and our Anasazi brethren who've ever known what's inside this mesa.

"But if people start talking about those rocks you found, pretty soon, there goes the neighborhood," the man said, returning to his entertainment voice. "So I had to get those bags of rocks you'd taken. Can't have any evidence of my little operation falling into the wrong hands.

"Unfortunately, I seemed to have missed a bag or two, and suddenly, everybody was talking about the remarkable gemstones found along the river.

"Well, so, enough!" the man said, replacing his chair against the wall. "We need to go on to other things, like what to do with you."

Mogi was slowly understanding how much he and the others threatened the man's plans.

"Why do you need to do anything with us? I'd be perfectly happy to completely forget that I ever met you," Jennifer said in a strong voice.

The man roared with laughter.

"Ah, a noble woman, willing to forget so quickly! Oh, I wish it was that easy. I really do. Just let you go, let bygones be bygones, travel our separate ways, parting with sweet sorrow, never again shall the twain meet.

"Unfortunately, that won't work," the man said in a matter-of-fact voice. "I believe that you have to die."

CHAPTER 18

The man jerked the four teenagers to their feet and shoved them down the stairway, lecturing them about the mine as they struggled to balance with their handcuffed hands.

"In the old days, it was just me and a couple of guys I hired for the hard labor—breaking off pieces of lava down in the pipe and hauling them to the tables where I could chip out the good stuff. It was hard finding people I could trust. I had to be careful who knew what was going on."

They reached the floor above the entrance tunnel.

"Turn right," the man commanded.

A worn path led to a lighted circular stairway in what looked like a vertical mine shaft. The man herded the four teens down the steps.

Jennifer, behind the other three, turned her head to talk. She couldn't help but be curious about why someone would put so much energy into such an evil plan.

"How in the world did you do all this?" she asked.

"We only work two or three months in the winter and spring. When Wonder Boy saw me, we were closing up for the season."

"Why only then?"

"This is wonderfully isolated country," the man said.

"But there're a lot of idiots on the river in the spring and summer, some even in September and October. We don't make a lot of noise, mostly working by hand with picks, but I'm not going to risk somebody hearing us."

The man was sounding again as if he were giving a lecture.

"I have to keep it that way to make sure that the location of the turquoise is never discovered. When the time is right to put it back into play, I'll say that one of my other mines hit a new vein and started bringing brand new turquoise right out of the shaft. It will, of course, actually be coming from my warehouses. If anyone discovered I was selling the Navajo Nation turquoise that was actually theirs to begin with, I'm afraid this little business of mine wouldn't work very well."

Jennifer kept asking questions, and the man continued to talk.

He had closed the mine at the time of the rafting trip when he realized Mogi had taken precious stones from the pool. Afterward, he paid close attention to what was written in the school newspaper, on school blogs, and on Facebook—including Mogi's waterfall picture posted by Mr. Jennings. It was obvious that any more attention to the gemstones would push someone to really question where they came from. He needed to get those rocks.

The break-in at the school was probably a mistake, the man admitted, and having Mogi walk into the middle of it was just bad luck. He had ransacked the geology lab to make it look like vandalism, but then an explosion of rage at seeing the picture made him break the trophy case glass. If anyone noticed a mysterious figure on the side of a mysterious mesa, things would only get worse.

Given all the publicity in the past, what was needed now was a diversion, something to make people forget about the rocks.

It was his good luck that she and her friends had come along. That made it easy to make something happen that would take all the attention away from the rocks, like some teenagers dying in a tragic rafting accident.

Downriver, of course. Far away from the stranded mesa.

That would take everybody's mind off the gemstones, and interest would soon drain away.

The circular stairway ended in a room the size of a single-car garage. Moving ahead, the man grabbed a bar attached to a wall, turned it several times, and gave the wall a push. A long, irregular crack of daylight appeared overhead and to the sides, then widened. As the light came in, the man moved to an electrical switch box on the wall and pulled a lever. As the soft whine of a generator decreased, the electric lights inside faded out.

The opening to the outside was about half the size of a house door. The man took a long piece of chain from a hook near the door and threaded it between their arms, then locked the ends together. It wouldn't do for anyone to try to run away. He moved them through the small door into the light.

Squinting in the bright sun, Mogi saw that they were at the top of the sloping side of the draw, much farther up the canyon than he and Frank had walked.

Forced to kneel on the ground a short distance from the door, Mogi turned and watched. The man pushed the door closed. It was as carefully fitted to the surrounding rock as the tunnel door on the ledge but was permanently hinged to the inside passageway. Kneeling close to the bottom, the man inserted a metal bar into a small hole and rotated it several times.

There was a sound of scraping metal as the locking mechanism rolled into place. He removed the bar, placed a rock over the small hole, then pressed his metal key into the sand, wiping away any mark made by his hand.

Moving from the wall, the man reached into a clump of bushes nearby and lifted a hidden pipe. The whole clump of bushes moved with him as he swung them directly in front of the stone door.

The doorway had vanished. There was no sign of a door, a passage, a stairway, a chamber, a mine, or any hidden Anasazi petroglyphs.

"I *am* good," he said as he yanked them to their feet again and started down the slope. Stumbling for almost a mile, they finally drew close to the river. As they neared the raft, a man sitting under a tree stood up.

"It's about time you got here," the man said.

It was Bill, the BLM ranger who had threatened the teens about the permit at Mr. Bottington's building.

"I tried to convince you dummies to stay away from the river," he snarled. "But, no, you had to play heroes, poking your noses where they don't belong. Well, now you're going to pay for it, big time."

The ranger removed the chain and, one by one, undid the captives' handcuffs long enough to take off their backpacks, force them into PFDs, shove them down into the front of Mr. Bottington's raft, and cuff them again with their arms looped around the safety rope attached around the top of the raft. He threw the backpacks in on top of them and the chain into the back of the raft.

The ladder was back in its awkward position, hanging over the front tube, though it was now dented and twisted. The ranger had probably used the hidden entrance on the ledge to kick it into the canyon below and then gone outside to drag it to the river. Pulled up next to the raft was a dull brown, inflatable two-person canoe. It was hardly noticeable against the bright red of the raft.

Looking at the shadows in the canyon and the brightness of the sun against the sandstone cliffs,

Mogi guessed that it was early afternoon. Doing the calculations in his head, he figured they had three or maybe even four hours before nightfall. Remembering the distances on his map, that would put them in the St. John's Canyon area, one of the campsites that the high school trip had used.

Thinking of the river after that, it suddenly occurred to him what was going to happen.

Government Rapid.

The worst rapid on the river, the one that Mr. Bottington had told them to carry the raft around, would be reached tomorrow. On the school trip, with experienced oarsmen, it was a fun ride with huge waves. With the water still high and someone rowing who had never rowed it before, the run was difficult and dangerous and probably would end with a turned-over raft. The passengers may be bashed into rocks, sucked into whirlpools, or drowned in churning water.

Government Rapid would be a perfect place for an accident.

That's how they'll do it, Mogi thought. They'll drown us first, then put us in the raft with our PFDs undone.

Pushing the raft into the current, ripping the tubes at the right moment, it would look like a bunch of dumb kids had pushed their luck and lost.

After the boss had stepped over the teenagers and gotten into his seat, Mr. Ranger shoved the raft into the water. Getting into the canoe and pushing it into the current, he paddled behind.

CHAPTER 19

"You shouldn't try anything foolish," Mr. Evil said as he held the oars steady in the water. "It's bad practice for passengers to be tied to the raft, but we wouldn't want anyone jumping out, would we? And I don't want you without your PFDs, that will come later.

"It's all in the timing, you know. Until then, all children not accompanied by a parent or legal guardian must have their flotation devices securely buckled.

"I am so funny!" he cackled.

Mogi and Becky were squashed together on the front floor of the raft on one side of the ladder, with Jennifer and Frank squeezed like them on the other side. For all of them, the handcuffs around the safety rope on top of the raft kept their bodies twisted and their arms raised in a painful position. No matter which way Mogi turned, his legs cramped repeatedly, and his back muscles were shot with spasms of pain.

"My wrists are killing me!" Jennifer screamed in a low voice to Becky.

Becky said nothing, only looking back with a face of fear. Even Frank was pale and breathing hard.

Mogi was horrified by what he had done. It was his fault. He had been intent on getting to the mesa, exploring the opening in the rock, and going on in spite of good sense saying not to. Now he had gotten them in a major mess, and he had to get them out. But how? He knew he wouldn't quit on them, but he couldn't escape the sense of doom—there was nothing he could do.

From the hard slap the man had given him, Mogi's lip had swelled to twice its normal size. Blood and spit dribbled down his chin and onto his T-shirt. The wound in his chest that the man had poked was throbbing like it had been torn open.

Trying to ignore his pains, Mogi watched the two men carefully, trying to find a weakness, any mistake they made, any opportunity to change the situation.

There seemed to be none. Since threatening them in the cavern, the man had kept his gun holstered on his belt and now was patiently moving the oars in the water, not wearing a PFD because it wouldn't fit over the holster. He was obviously an experienced oarsman, but Mogi could hear him quietly cursing the ladder that projected off the front of the raft. It made it hard to see ahead and caused the raft to wallow in the water instead of gliding smoothly.

Ranger Bill, keeping about fifty feet behind the

raft, watched the man and his captives while glancing side-to-side, staying aware.

It was hopeless.

———

Mr. Evil aimed the raft toward the shore and rowed hard into the bank. Sliding over the side into the shallow water, he pulled the boat up and tied it to a boulder on the beach. The ranger pulled the canoe up next to the raft and clipped it to the rope with its bottom halfway out of the water.

They were at the St. John's Canyon campsite.

The teens were uncuffed, taken from the raft, and shoved up the shore into a thicket of willows. Then the two men took the chain from the raft, handcuffed the four again, and ran the chain between their arms and around two thick trunks.

Even still shackled, it was a relief to lie down, stretch their legs, rest their backs, and rub their necks. They whispered anxiously to each other but found no relief, no new ideas of how to escape, no hope anything was going to change.

While the four friends huddled close, Mr. Evil and the ranger threw the dry bags to the shore, then lifted out the cooler and carried it up to the campsite. Ranger Bill opened the cooler and yanked out some packages.

"I hope they put in something decent to eat," the boss man said. "If it's all Gummy Bears, I'm going to drown every one of them right now."

To his delight, he found that the teenagers had packed sandwich makings and drinks, and Mr. Bottington had contributed a tin of homemade cookies, the ingredients for breakfast burritos, a coffee pot to boil water, and packets of hot chocolate. The two men were soon eating their fill.

The evening was uneventful. Being handcuffed to the chain was better than the boat, but the captives couldn't adjust their positions, scratch themselves, or brush off insects and lizards.

And there were things they needed.

Can we have our sleeping bags? Can I have some water? I'm hungry. Do we get to eat something? I need to pee. I want my jacket. Can we have the cookies?

Mr. Evil uncoupled the teenagers one by one and led them into the bushes to relieve themselves. The ranger grudgingly used the lunch meats to make burritos for the starving captives but refused to light the stove. Keeping two of the sleeping bags for himself and his boss, he unzipped the others and threw them over the four bodies crammed together for warmth. The teens used their PFDs as pillows.

It was enough to get them to darkness, and the camp settled into a somewhat awkward but adequate sleep.

———

Mogi never closed his eyes, nor did he hear regular breathing from his friends beside him. He was waiting until the time was right, and the time seemed right at around two in the morning. Deep breathing from one man and snoring from the other was a good signal.

"Becky," Mogi whispered to Jennifer, who whispered to Becky. "Let me have a barrette."

Puzzled, Becky took a thin metal barrette from her hair and handed it to Mogi, who immediately started bending the bottom back and forth. When it broke, he snapped the paired tines in two. Then he looked at the smallest piece in the moonlight, straightened it with his teeth, and stuck it in the metal slit of his handcuffs where the teeth met. The cuffs slid open.

Jennifer looked at him with surprised eyes.

"YouTube," he mouthed back.

One by one, moving slow and being absolutely quiet, he opened the cuffs of the others. Quickly and silently, they slipped out from under the chain, grabbed their PFDs, and moved slowly down the path to the beach.

Mogi bunched up the sleeping bags as if they still covered bodies, then followed his comrades.

Moving low and slow, trying to attract no attention even if one of the men glanced up, the four crept carefully away from the camp and through the rocks, weeds, and bushes until they reached the river's shore. Slipping on their PFDs, they slid quietly into the water.

CHAPTER 20

Even knowing they couldn't be heard over the noise of the river, Mogi, Jennifer, Becky, and Frank talked in low voices and only when bunched together in the current.

A mile down the river, they allowed themselves to smile and pound Mogi on the back. They were in the middle of a river in the middle of the night, but they'd escaped and were appreciating their freedom. The moon was bright enough to show them the river and its shores.

"Okay, whiz kid," Jennifer said. "Why were you looking at YouTube to learn how to get out of handcuffs?"

Mogi laughed. "Somebody shared a video that showed it on Facebook. I just thought it was interesting. Do you know there are hundreds of videos showing how to get out of things?"

"What now?" Becky asked, not interested in handcuffs.

Jennifer grabbed Mogi's PFD and gave it a jerk, a clear indication he should remain silent.

She turned to Becky. "I figure we've got three or four hours at best before they wake up. I remember Mr. Bottington talking about the river flowing at five or six miles an hour, and I figure we'll be doing good to get half that.

"That means we could be as far as twelve miles downriver before they start. Once those guys do start, though, they'll be rowing maybe twice or three times as fast as we're going.

"We'll make it past Government Rapid and into the slow part of the river before we see them. After that, the river is so slow we'll be able to get out and run on the sand bars. It'll be a lot faster. I'm betting we'll make it to Mr. Bottington long before they do."

Mogi started again to say something, but Jennifer again looked sternly at her brother. As the twins swam ahead, when she figured they couldn't hear, she held onto his PFD and spoke directly into his ear.

"I didn't want you to tell them that the canoe would be faster."

Even if only one man rode in the canoe while the other rowed the raft, that one man could go much faster than the river's current. He would be on them much sooner than Jennifer's calculations.

"I wanted them to have something to hope for," she said, then added, "I wanted me to have something to hope for."

Mogi nodded. "I'm sorry. I didn't mean for this to

happen, but I'll get us out of this, okay? I will. I promise."

She patted his PFD and then let go, swimming into the current to join the twins.

They all kept paddling in the water, sometimes swimming, sometimes floating, sometimes using a backstroke.

As they randomly switched positions, it was obvious it was an effort that favored skill and long arms.

Jennifer was the smoothest, even with the bulk of the clumsy PFD. She was a natural swimmer, and her brother had arms at least four inches longer than hers. With those advantages, there wasn't much hope for the twins to keep up. Mogi remembered Frank talking about the absence of water in the Lukachukai Mountains of his home. It must have been only at public pools that they'd experienced any deep water at all.

Everyone was also getting tired.

"Let's try something," Mogi said, waiting for everyone to come together. "Turn over on your backs and open the last buckle on your PFD."

They did what he said.

Then he pulled Becky between Frank's legs and clipped his buckle onto the belt strap at the back of her jacket. After that, he buckled Jennifer's last buckle onto Frank's strap, and then his onto hers.

"Okay, fold your legs around the person in front of you, lay back, and use a backstroke. Our arms are stronger that way, and if you get tired, stop and relax for a minute. This will keep all of us together."

It was clumsy to begin with, but with Mogi calling out a cadence, the arms were soon working together, and though they looked like an upside-down caterpillar, the teens' progress was steady. Mogi watched over his shoulders to keep them in the middle of the current and away from the banks.

It made for a long night, but it worked.

———

Dawn arrived and then sunlight, and the four teenagers were worn out. Worse, they could see now by looking at the shore how pitifully slow they seemed to be moving. It was discouraging, but their spirits more than soared when they heard, then saw, Government Rapid ahead.

They had covered a good number of miles since their escape and were within a mile or two of the shallows!

No one even considered running the rapid, though it would have shot them down the canyon much faster than walking around. But as they got out of the water and moved quickly down the well-worn path around the dangerous rapid, they looked back.

Far in the distance, a brown canoe had appeared, the man inside paddling furiously.

That sent the four of them scrambling, running down the path beyond the rapid and along the shore until the path ran out. After that, it was back in the water.

They passed around a bend of the canyon and into the slow stretches of the river, never having seen the canoe come through Government Rapid. A rough guess gave them another hour before the canoe would catch up.

If only they could hold out.

CHAPTER 21

The stair-step pattern of the canyon walls had given way to more vertical cliffs, making the river more confined between its walls. The river itself, coming into a part where sediment had backed into the narrow channel, slowed because it was leveling out and meandered now from one side of the corridor to the other. The sun had been up an hour or so, but the morning was still cool, and being in the water and the shade made the four escapees shiver.

On each side of the river, the ground sloping from the bottom of the cliffs, a thinner strip than where the canyon was wider, was full of boulders, weeds, cactus, and an almost-continuous run of heavily leaved tamarisk trees. If there had been a path along the slopes, the four teens would have been happy to walk and run the rest of the way out.

But there was no path. The sandbars that had

developed with the slower water and flatter channel offered the only relief from their caterpillar paddling.

The four exhausted youths crawled up the edges of the first sand bar and trotted across the dry sand, happy to be free of the water. When the river curved across the canyon in front of them, the sandbar disappeared, then suddenly appeared on the other side. They waded into the water, then swam quickly across.

Their efforts were good for a time—wading, swimming, and bullying their way across a dozen sandbars. But their bodies had had little water and food for more than a day. Dehydration was taking its toll.

Reaching one sandbar and struggling up the side, they all collapsed and looked upriver. Behind them, the canoe—once far in the distance—was drawing closer.

"We've got to go," Mogi urged. "Get up! Get up! We've got to move."

Becky sat sucking air. Playing Rezball in the Navajo school basketball league, she'd been a center because she was stouter than the others. She wasn't made for long-distance running.

Frank, with Mogi's legs a half-foot longer than his, was taking many more steps just to keep up. Now he was exhausted.

The others didn't move, no matter what Mogi urged.

Mogi didn't know what to do. He had strength to keep running—thank God for basketball—but couldn't leave the others. He watched dejectedly as the canoe steadily gained on them, not more than a few hundred yards away now, still in the current. He could see that it was Ranger Bill. But what if he had the pistol now? A bullet hole in a drowned body would be a clear sign of foul play, so Mogi was sure Mr. Evil's plan was still to catch the four of them and create an *accident* that would be convincing enough to fool people. But time was running out. If it was the only alternative to being caught, Mogi was sure that the men would shoot them and sink their bodies.

They were so close to safety, he said to himself, looking up at the tall walls of rock around him. The ragged shape of the cliff tops and the curve of the river, as he looked down the canyon, were familiar. He remembered this place but couldn't recall why.

They were near the end, maybe another eight or nine miles to where Mr. Bottington expected to meet them.

Was he there already? When would he start worrying about them? What would he do if they never came?

Mogi looked again at the canoe in the distance. The man must be tired too, as he was stroking more slowly, leaning forward and laboring with the paddle. That meant that Mr. Evil was in the raft. It was much slower, but it would be coming all the same. Ranger Bill had only to catch them, hold them, and wait.

Mogi's eyes drifted up the high walls and back to the riverbed in front of him. Why did it look so familiar?

"Up! Up!" he was suddenly yelling. "Give me ten more minutes! Just ten more. We can do it. Jennifer, help me get them up!"

His sudden urgency rallied the others, and, struggling through the pain in their legs, the four began trotting down the remaining length of their sandbar. Again, the river zigzagged to their side of the canyon, and they slid into the water, laboring to push through to the next sandbar.

When they got there, it was different. There was no sharp edge of dry sand but instead a shallow, dark rim of wetness around it.

"Do what I do! Everybody! Do what I do!"

Mogi's urging seemed strange. Then it was even stranger when he laid down on the edge as he reached the new sandbar, and started rolling his body across the wet sand.

"Do what I did! Lay down and roll! Now!"

The others were too tired not to obey. Half-falling, half-heaving their bodies, they each rolled the ten feet to where Mogi was.

"Okay, everybody into the bushes. Find a boulder and get behind it."

Jennifer looked at him with exhaustion. "He'll just find us, Mogi. It's no good to hide. He's probably got the gun."

Mogi grabbed her arm and helped her up. "You gotta do it. Get somewhere and stay down."

As his friends struggled to the sloping ground next to the cliffs, Mogi fell to his knees, not more than twenty feet from the edge of the sandbar.

The effect on the canoeist of seeing them do this was noticeable. Ranger Bill dug his paddle into the water and pushed his craft into a sprint, ready to end the chase.

As the canoe picked up speed, Mogi slowly backed up on the sandbar toward the shore, making sure not to go too fast. When the canoe hit the sandbar, he dashed into the bushes.

The boat bumped hard into the shore, and Ranger Bill launched himself over the side of the canoe. He pulled Mr. Evil's holster and gun from next to the seat and strapped it around his waist, then pulled the canoe onto the sand. A determined grin on his face, he hurried up the sandbar.

He got to the dark area and made it a few steps before his boots began to sink.

The ranger struggled, yanking at his legs to get them out of the mud, but he only sank faster, the mud gurgling up, around, and over his boots and up his legs. He leaned over, trying to roll onto his side, but the mud held fast, keeping him upright.

Screaming in frustration, he tried to power his way out but could make no progress.

He was stuck.

He tried to go backward to the canoe but could not move that way either. The boat, only two arm lengths away, was out of reach.

Enraged, he pulled out his gun and fired toward the teens in the bushes.

Damn! Damn! Damn!

Breathing hard, hating everything around him, slapping his hands against the mud that had grabbed him so hard, and finally screaming at the air above him, the man slumped back onto the surface of the wet mud, caught so embarrassingly by something with a dumb name like Whale's Blubber.

———

Mogi had watched the man through the dense tamarisk as he foundered, then smiled at Jennifer, Becky, and Frank, all safely tucked behind boulders.

"Hey, Bill," Mogi yelled.

The response was an explosive string of expletives.

"So, Bill," Mogi continued. "I don't think you're going to get out of that mud. Throw the gun over to us and we'll pull you out."

There was another string of expletives.

"Hey, Bill," Jennifer called out, "I don't think you've thought this through. See all this heavy vegetation running along the river? You already can't see us, so I bet we could sneak off and leave you stuck in the mud. Your boss will be along pretty soon, but he'll realize he should get off this river as soon as he can, which means he won't be interested in stopping to help you out of the mud."

There was silence from the stuck man, who'd restarted his efforts to pull his legs out.

"I'll sweeten the pot, Bill," Mogi said. "You throw us the gun, we'll pull you out, and then we'll give you a head start in the canoe. You'll beat your boss off the river in a couple of hours. That's even before we could make it back to town. You could be miles away before the sheriff knows to look for you."

The man stopped his struggles.

It took about five minutes.

"Okay, but I want that head start," the ranger finally said.

"Toss the gun toward the bushes."

The man did as he was told.

Mogi waited a couple of minutes, then dashed out, picked up the revolver, signaled to Jennifer, and walked out onto the sandbar.

"Hey! Come get me out of this!" the trapped man yelled.

Mogi moved slowly toward him. He kept the ranger's attention until Jennifer had quietly moved upriver along the shore, slipped into the water unnoticed, drifted behind the canoe, pulled it off the mud, pointed it downriver, and swam with it alongside the sandbar.

"Hey!"

"Well, Bill," Mogi said as Becky and Frank came up next to him, "I forgot that we really need that canoe. I'm sure sorry. We'll send someone back to get you."

The three teenagers headed toward Jennifer. They still had a lot of river to go.

———

Less than an hour later, with Jennifer and Becky paddling the canoe, Frank crammed between them, and Mogi jogging on the sand where he could, they heard a puttering sound as a small raft-like boat appeared ahead of them.

It was Mr. Bottington.

The old river horse was a patient and trusting man and believed young people needed the freedom to adventure on their own. But that ladder had continued to sit uncomfortably with him, and he had decided his help might be needed.

Early that morning, he'd loaded a trailer with a hard-bottomed raft he reserved for emergencies. It was four feet shorter than the raft Mogi and his friends had used and had smaller tubes and a back-board across the rear. A small gas-powered outboard motor fit onto the board and let Mr. Bottington go upriver against the current. The motor and boat were small enough to be carried separately around any rapid, permitting him, with moderate effort, to access the whole river if he had to.

Motors were not officially permitted on the river, but guides and rangers were allowed to use them for rescues under emergency conditions—and that was what Mr. Bottington feared he might be undertaking.

It had taken him two hours to get to the take-out spot on the river and another thirty minutes to get everything rigged.

So now he was coming toward the four teenagers at a good clip, his face showing how happy he was to see them all safe but full of wonder at why they had a brown canoe rather than a red raft.

Either way, the four teens were whooping and yelling, waving and laughing.

It took several minutes—several long minutes—for them to tell the full story, and Mr. Bottington was hesitant to believe it all. A huge hidden chamber in an isolated mesa with a secret turquoise mine and two men who were planning on murdering the teens was a little much to take in all at once.

Deciding to leave the details for later, Mogi beached the canoe on a sandbar and joined the others with Mr. Bottington as he continued to motor up the river. It was a tight fit for the five of them, but no one was about to be left behind.

It was only ten minutes to Ranger Bill, who had continued his struggle against the mud and was even more trapped as a result.

Mr. Bottington waved as they passed.

Puttering through a number of curves in the river, the rescue raft finally rounded a corner into faster current, and the motor fought harder to make progress. Those onboard peered ahead as Government Rapid soon came into view.

It looked different.

As soon as there was a path along the shore, Mr. Bottington pulled over and tied the boat to a boulder. Cautiously, the five of them walked the path to the bottom of the rapid.

The waves were still large, the sound pounding in their ears, and the spray from the water crashing against the rocks carried into the breeze around them.

But the middle of the rapid was a scene of destruction.

An extension ladder leaned halfway across the churning foam, bent and twisted, as half of the red raft rose out of the water next to it, pressed up against a huge rock by the power of the water. One of the tubes had burst and fluttered now as the waves swept across it.

There was no one to be seen.

Mr. Bottington described what must have happened, using his hands to illustrate what the raft looked like as it came into the rapid.

"He gave it a good try, I would guess, but that ladder just makes the raft behave in all sorts of bad ways. It makes the front tube dip into a wave instead of over it, so the raft takes on water and swings sideways, and if the ladder hits a rock at the same time, which is what I guess happened, it punctures the floor and holds the raft under water long enough for the river to shove it against the rock. The current pins it and won't let it move after that.

"Whoever was oaring the boat would have been thrown into the whole mess."

"The man didn't have a PFD on," Mogi shouted above the noise. "It didn't fit over his pistol."

"Well, I expect that he wished he had."

Mr. Bottington used a satellite phone in his boat to call the river rangers. There was no point waiting for them, and he wanted to get the kids back to town

—they were dehydrated, bruised, bloody, and exhausted.

The real rangers were there by afternoon, using winches and cables to pull what remained of the raft onto the shore. They unsnagged the ladder and picked up Ranger Bill on the way out.

They found Mr. Evil's body the next day.

CHAPTER 22

Mogi and the others found it hard to believe, but Jacob Theodore Crampton had been a well-respected resident of Tucson, Arizona, a gentleman in his business dealings with just the right measure of ambition.

He was, indeed, a wealthy man, known for his generosity and good humor.

A full investigation of his gemstone holdings and business practices, however, pieced together a picture of a power-hungry murderer. The story held the newspaper headlines for weeks. Ultimately, a dozen *accidental* deaths at his mines, shops, and warehouses revealed a man without a conscience, a man who had turned to evil with a passion.

After being treated as a crime scene by the tribal police and FBI, the secret mesa was opened to select government and tribal officials, plus a few reporters. Pictures of its hidden chamber appeared in newspapers as far away as London and Singapore. Even as

archaeologists claimed the mesa as a national trea-
sure, the Navajo Nation was not swayed—it was
clearly theirs. Northern Arizona University in
Flagstaff argued—unsuccessfully—for partial rights
since one of its professors had found the site in the
first place.

Crampton and his workers had looted the Anasazi
artifacts, selling every pot, mat, and grinding stone to
private collectors who didn't ask questions. Even so,
the cavern and its petroglyphs were expected to hold
enough mysteries to absorb researchers for years.

Immediate plans were on the drawing board to
open it as a tourist attraction, with the number of
visitors projected to rival Monument Valley. Someone
had already done a quick sketch of a hotel complex
with a massive swinging bridge from the rim of the
canyon to the top of the mesa, and it was only one
idea of dozens.

Crampton's warehouses provided truckloads of
turquoise, removed from the hidden mesa as well as
other mines in the Southwest. Many of the region's
tribes argued for ownership of some part of the pile,
and it was finally decided that a committee under the
Bureau of Indian Affairs should work out a just distribution of the stones.

Mogi's mother and father reimbursed Mr.
Bottington for the loss of his raft and equipment, but
Mogi and Jennifer had to earn the money to replace
the family's ladder.

Becky and Frank were promised college scholar-
ships by the Navajo Nation Council, and the towns of

Bluff and Mexican Hat held a special ceremony for all four teenagers, as well as for Burl Bottington, naming him Citizen of the Year for his willingness to trust the next generation of young people. As rewarding a recognition as that was, Burl was most pleased when a Salt Lake City restaurant named its all-you-can-eat prime rib special the *Bottington Bonanza*.

———

"You climb up here for the fun of it?" Becky asked with a breathless voice. "You're nuts."

"I'm with you," Jennifer echoed. "His mind is more twisted than I thought."

Mogi had attached a rope to the platform to make things easier, but it still took several careful minutes for him, his sister, Becky, and Frank to make their way up the cliff, along the narrow ledge, and around the corner into the alcove. From there, he showed them how to crawl into the hidden room in the back. The visitors looked with amazement at the tall cylinder of stone reaching far above them.

It was summer, and Frank and Becky were soon to return to their own mountains and canyons. The Navajo Nation had convinced the BIA it should be allowed to use the gemstones that clearly came from the hidden mesa even before the larger distribution of the rest. A tribal committee, which included Frank and Becky's father, made sure every established Navajo jeweler received enough stone to work with for now, hoping to kick-start the economy across the reservation. The plan was an immediate success, as all the national publicity about the mesa caused a sudden and overwhelming demand for turquoise and silver rings, earrings, bracelets, and necklaces.

Wanting to do something before the twins left, Mogi planned a special day, and what could be more special than to take them to his most special place?

"I have a gift for you," Frank said as they sat around the small space of the inner room. He reached into his daypack and took out a box wrapped in corn-husks and tied with a leather strap. Shyly smiling, he handed it to Mogi.

Mogi carefully undid the strap and neatly folded back the husks. Opening the box, he found a solid silver bracelet decorated with a wide band of turquoise inlaid from one side to the other, polished to a mirrored surface. It was a beautiful deep blue with tiny filigrees of gold like a fine spider web through the soft curves.

"My dad says that it's the most unique turquoise ever found, worth more than any other kind. And it's a big deal now that the Nation has a source of stones on the reservation itself. They named it Navajo San Juan Turquoise."

Mogi fit it around his left wrist. Looking at the depth of the color, the fineness of the filigree, and the flawless gleam of the silver, he held it up to his cheek and felt the smoothness. It was impressive.

"And I have a gift for you," Becky said as she faced Jennifer. "My grandmother suggested it. She has heard me tell of your love for life and for your brother." From her pack, she took a long, thin, white box tied with a small piece of rawhide strip and placed it on Jennifer's lap.

Jennifer couldn't keep back her tears. She carefully undid the rawhide tie and gently opened the box. Between two layers of the softest, whitest deerskin she had ever seen lay a long, delicate feather, shining a golden brown against its white blanket. Tied to the feather was a small bear carved out of Navajo San Juan turquoise.

"This is an eagle feather that has been with my grandfather for many years," Becky said, "considered by him to be a source of courage and inner power. If you hold it next to your heart, it will help bring harmony to your life. My grandfather listened to our stories, and he believes that you have the spirit of an eagle inside.

"I want you to hold the feather next to your heart when you think of us," Becky said as she took it out of the buckskin and wrapped Jennifer's hand around it.

"Think of us often."

Mogi waited for Jennifer to return the feather to the box, then finally said, "Okay. Let's dance."

The four friends stood. With Mogi behind Frank and Jennifer behind Becky, Mogi's phone began playing the beat of Navajo drums he had downloaded the day before.

The Navajo twins led their friends in a rhythmic dance.

Mogi and Jennifer learned the emphasis of the first beat of the measure, the long shuffles, when to turn, when to reverse. When the Franklins had mastered some of the footwork, Frank and Becky added their voices, chanting to the spirits of their ancestors.

The deep thump of the Indian drums carried up the narrow shaft of stone to the sky. The sound resonated as the massive hollow tube amplified it and sent its rhythm around the landscape of stone. If anyone elsewhere in that empty land who heard the mystical beats stopped to listen—turning one way, then another to locate the origin—they would only find that the music surrounded them, like a spirit in the wind.

A LOOK AT: THE LOST CHILDREN

THE MOGI FRANKLIN MYSTERY
SERIES 2

Unlock the Secrets of the Past in *The Lost Children*—A Thrilling Middle-Grade Mystery Adventure!

In 1891, three children disappeared into the forest during a mountain picnic and were never seen again. Over a century later, Mogi Franklin and his sister, Jennifer, stumble upon clues that could finally solve the mystery. But when a greedy billionaire threatens to destroy an entire town to build an exclusive resort, Mogi and Jennifer's quest for answers becomes even more dangerous.

As they unravel the secrets of the past, Mogi's sharp problem-solving skills are put to the ultimate test. Can he outsmart a ruthless tycoon, save a town, and uncover what really happened to the lost children?

The Lost Children is the second thrilling installment in the *Mogi Franklin Mystery* series, perfect for middle-grade readers who love fast-paced adventures, historical mysteries, and clever heroes.

AVAILABLE DECEMBER 2024

ABOUT THE AUTHOR

New Mexico-based Don Willerton is the author of *Death in the Tallgrass*, the winner of the Western Writers of America 2024 SPUR Award for Western Historical Fiction, a finalist in the 2024 American Fiction Awards, and a finalist in the 2024 Storytrade Book Awards. He has written a ten-book Middle Grade/Young Adult mystery series located in the Southwest, two contemporary thrillers, and a fictional World War II adventure novel.

To finance his writing, he used his degrees in physics and computer science as a scientist, manager, and computer specialist, but has always let his curiosity, imagination, and passion for history keep his head aligned with his heart.